PRIMAL 2055 QUEST

JACK SILKSTONE

VINCI BOOKS

By Jack Silkstone

PRIMAL 2055

PRIMAL 2055 — Escape
PRIMAL 2055 — Quest

The Primal Series

PRIMAL Origin
PRIMAL Unleashed
PRIMAL Vengeance
PRIMAL Fury
PRIMAL Reckoning
PRIMAL Nemesis
PRIMAL Redemption
PRIMAL Renegade
PRIMAL Deception
PRIMAL Exodus

SEAL

SEAL of Approval
SEAL the Deal
Signed SEAL'd and Delivered

Standalone

The Operative

Vinci Books

vinci-books.com

Published by Vinci Books Ltd in 2026

1

Copyright © Jack Silkstone 2020

The author has asserted their moral right to be identified as the author of this work in accordance with the Copyright, Designs and Patents Act 1988. This work is a work of fiction. Names, characters, places and incidents are the product of the author's imagination or are used fictitiously. Any resemblance to actual persons, living or dead, places and incidents is entirely coincidental.

All rights reserved. No part of this publication may be copied, reproduced, distributed, stored in any retrieval system, or transmitted in any form or by any means, including photocopying, recording, or other electronic or mechanical methods, nor used as a source for any form of machine learning including AI datasets, without the prior written permission of the publisher.

The publisher and the author have made every effort to obtain permissions for any third party material used in this book and to comply with copyright law. Any queries in this respect should be brought to the attention of the publisher and any omissions will be corrected in future editions.

A CIP catalogue record for this book is available from the British Library.

Paperback ISBN: 9781036703837

The EU GPSR authorised representative is Logos Europe, 9 rue Nicolas Poussion, 17000 La Rochelle, France contact@logoseurope.eu

Chapter One

Western Desert, Iraq

Wilda grimaced as she sat, bracing herself against the warm metal of the truck bed. The wound in her flank sent jolts of pain through her battered body. She sucked air through clenched teeth and slid herself to the rear of the vehicle. Swinging her feet to the ground she ignored the pain and gathered her thoughts.

It had been five days since she and the others had made their escape from the Sakkin prison in the city of Homs. Five days since Wilda, a sixteen-year-old trainee had betrayed her masters and escaped. Five days since a missile had killed her only friend, Henry.

Wiping a tear from the corner of her eye she gazed out at the horizon where the faint glow of the sun was fading. A cool breeze ruffled her hair, the first sign of another freezing night.

Moving stiffly past the truck she spotted people clustered around a small fire. The others had circled their vehicles for the night and were preparing the evening meal. Walking tentatively toward them she caught a whiff of roasting meat. The smell triggered a savage growl from her stomach.

One of them turned toward her as she hobbled closer. She saw Xeyal break away from the group with a bowl in hand. The twelve-year-old had been acting as her nurse since the small convoy had left Homs. Every time she'd woken, the girl with curly brown hair had been there to wipe her brow, wet her lips and help the doctor dress her wounds.

"Wilda, you should be resting. I was bringing you food," said Xeyal as she reached her.

"I needed to get out of that truck," she replied as she continued toward the others and the fire.

Xeyal's brother Behdin, rose from where he was sitting with his Dragunov rifle, and offered her his place on a wooden crate. Only two years older than his sister, the boy's dark eyes already bore the intensity that came from exposure to the savagery of conflict.

"How are you feeling?" he asked as she sat.

"Better."

Xeyal handed her a bowl. "You should eat. Behdin shot a goat."

Spooning the thick stew into her mouth she was pleasantly surprised by the rich flavors. "This is good," she managed between mouthfuls.

As she ate, other members of their convoy filed past the fire for a bowl of the stew. There were less than a dozen refugees, all adults, and all armed. They avoided making eye contact with her, and the ones that did wore a cautious look that bordered on fear. In their eyes, despite playing a pivotal role in their freedom, she was still a product of Sakkin, and Sakkin was the enemy.

Finishing her stew she left the fire and made her way back to the truck. Leaning against the hood she searched the northeastern horizon for an old friend. The Guardian Star was a beacon that called to her over the vastness of the desert, guiding her toward distant mountains and the facility nestled within them; the place from her dreams.

Fatigue washed over her, and she turned to the rear of the truck. Then, as she hobbled toward the tailgate, she heard something that turned her blood to ice.

The breeze carried the faint whirr of a drone's blades to her genetically enhanced ears.

"Take cover!" she screamed as her acute hearing also detected the distant roar of a vertjet.

As she dove to the ground railer projectiles slammed into the truck with a mighty clang. Then the attacking jet roared overhead and disappeared into the night. A glance toward the other vehicles confirmed they'd been immobilized in that first attack. Her training told her what would come next.

Pain shot through her body as she rose and staggered to the truck. It was still intact. Railer rounds had punched through the engine, leaving the body undamaged. Pushing aside a tattered canvas cover she reached for a crate and dragged it rearward. Inside she found the equipment that Behdin had squirreled away for her, body armor and an AKX assault rifle.

Unable to raise her left arm she lifted the armor over her head, tore the side of the vest open, and slid her right arm through the hole. Slapping the velcro closed she gripped the enhanced AK between her knees, shoved a magazine home, and racked the charging handle.

The first crackle of gunfire sounded in the desert to her

right. It was followed by the tell-tale hiss of railers and the wet slap of a human disintegrating.

Steadying the AK against the truck she scanned the sky through the weapon's enhanced optic. A fusing of thermal and night vision revealed the presence of a single Hunter drone. Sakkin operating procedures stipulated that at least one of the disc-shaped autonomous vehicles would be supporting an assault by three clankers and a ganic. Clankers, or mechops as Sakkin designated them, were robots capable of limited independent combat. Because of this they were led by a 'ganic', a highly trained human. Eliminating that individual was the most effective way to defeat a Sakkin attack. But first, she needed to deprive the assault force of their eyes.

The AKX barked twice, spitting its programmable bullets into the dark sky. Through the scope, she saw the flash of a hit and watched the drone drop.

Before it struck the ground she was on the move, hobbling alongside the truck. It wouldn't protect from Sakkin railers, but would hide her from their thermal sensors.

Crouching behind the shattered engine block she ignored the thick stench of oil and fuel as she peered around the bumper.

Her heart lurched as she spotted dark mounds where moments before people had stood eating their dinner. Beyond them she saw shadowy figures approaching, clankers. She waited till they were a short distance from the fire before she lined one up and fired. The advanced rounds punched a cluster of holes in the robot's sensor array and it blundered off at right angles to the assault.

Dropping to the ground she braced herself as a volley

of ultra high-velocity slugs rang the shattered truck like a bell.

Wilda's body was wracked with pain as she crawled away toward another truck. She'd almost reached it when the vehicle she'd left exploded in a flash of flame that lit up the sky. Debris rained down around her as she scrambled behind the remaining truck and rolled under it. Crawling to the opposite side she had a clear view of where her friends had gathered, only moments earlier.

In the flickering light of the fire she saw Behdin's lifeless eyes staring at her. She choked back tears as she searched for the enemy. A clanker appeared a mere twenty yards distant, an ominous figure that blocked the stars on the horizon.

Her AK barked as she sent a stream of armor-piercing rounds into the head of the robot. Bullets sparked against the active camouflage that cloaked the high-tech killing machine.

She changed magazines as she scrambled rearward, out from under the truck. Clambering to her feet she worked the cocking handle.

Over the low roar of a burning truck she registered the crunch of a heavy footfall behind her. Spinning she caught a glimpse of a figure before a flash of blue energy overwhelmed her vision. She lost control of her limbs as the ultrasonic wave disrupted the neurons controlling her muscles.

As she collapsed, the figure stood over her. The Sakkin operative's faceplate opened, revealing the features of someone she knew, Tree. The two of them had been trainees together. What's more, he'd once saved her life with a simple act of compassion.

"I'm sorry, Eight Two, but loose ends need to be tied up," was the last thing she heard before passing out.

When she came to she was strapped to a stretcher being loaded into an aircraft. It was the Sakkin vertjet that had strafed the convoy. She glimpsed more figures inside as her stretcher was locked into place. The ramp closed with a whine, and the aircraft lurched skyward.

"I told you I'd find you."

She instantly recognized the voice and turned her head till she faced the molten features of Sakkin trainee Seven Nine Nine.

"You killed them all," she managed between gritted teeth. "You killed them all."

He smirked. "That's just the beginning, Eight Two."

He disappeared, and for a few minutes she felt the aircraft bank and weave before it slowed then touched down.

Wilda's heart raced as two mechops carried her stretcher clear of the aircraft, and into a building she recognized. She'd seen it over and over in her dreams. It was the hospital where she'd been born.

Her stretcher was transferred to a gurney, and she was wheeled along a corridor, through several sliding doors into a brightly lit room.

Figures gathered around, and a machine hummed as a clamp grasped either side of her head.

"Welcome home," said a feminine voice. A face appeared in front of Wilda, the beautiful elfin features of a woman she'd seen once before, inside the Sakkin training facility.

"Why am I here?" Wilda asked. "Why not kill me with the others?"

The woman smiled. "Because my dear child, you have

something that belongs to us." The buzzing of a machine gained in intensity. She struggled to move her head. Cold metal touched the side of her temple, followed by intense pain as it commenced drilling into her skull.

Wilda's screams echoed off the walls of the facility as she thrashed against her restraints. Then, as the medical tool punched through her skull, she fell still.

Village Of Pendro, Kurdistan

Wilda clapped a hand to the side of her head as she sat upright, heart racing. Pain shot across her body, and she slumped back onto the bed, breathing heavily.

She wasn't in the hands of Sakkin, her friends weren't dead, and no one was drilling into her skull. Instead, she was lying injured in a stone shepherd's hut on the outskirts of Behdin and Xeyal's village.

Unlike the dream, their convoy had crossed the desert without being attacked. Behdin's story of their escape from Sakkin had ensured his family welcomed her, but the other villagers kept their distance. She didn't blame them. Life in the Morass was hard, and strangers couldn't always be trusted, especially ones linked to the forces that abducted their children.

Exhaling, she fought through the pain in her side as she slid off the mattress onto her knees. Leaning on the wall she made it to her feet and stood for a moment in the darkness.

The wound she'd sustained in combat with Seven Nine Nine should have killed her. Fighting on a rubble-strewn rooftop in Homs, a railer bolt had ripped through her torso, ripping muscles and devastating organs. However, somehow her body had been able to keep her alive and repair. She suspected it had something to do with the treatment she'd received in the *Institute*. Sakkin Industries had led the world in genetic research and manipulation. It made sense that their ganics would be enhanced. The thought sent a shiver up her spine as she wondered how much of her the corporation had changed.

Wilda felt along the wall until she found her jacket. Shrugging it on she found the walking stick that Behdin had carved for her and pushed open the rickety wooden door.

Icy wind whipped her hair as she scanned the darkness. The faintest glow of light from the east told her it was early morning. At least a dozen lights flickered from the village, a few hundred yards away. The people of Pendro were early risers.

She heard a faint cry from Behdin and Xeyal's house, fifty yards distant. Light shone from the girl's room. There wasn't a night that the child didn't wake screaming. Her dreams were every bit as real as Wilda's. It broke her heart that she couldn't help, but only a mother's embrace could soothe the child's anguish.

Behind the hut was a path that led up into the rocky slopes of a mountain range. She hiked it most mornings, in the hope it would help rehabilitate her wounded body. It also gave her time away from the village to think and, more importantly, remember.

Branches and thorns scraped at the shoulders of her jacket as she followed the goat trail through thick bushes. As she climbed, she wondered how dark it was to people without genetic enhancement. On the journey across the desert, she'd realized she could see details that Behdin, Xeyal and the others couldn't.

When she finally reached the edge of the thicket she

glanced up at the mountain. Toward the peak, the first rays of sunrise cast a wide swath of light across the craggy landscape.

She climbed a few hundred feet to an outcrop that overlooked the valley, and lowered herself gently onto a boulder. This was the part of the day she loved the most. Training underground in the Sakkin facility called the *Institute*, it was rare for Wilda to see the sun, let alone watch it rise over a majestic mountain range and spread its warmth across a fertile valley.

The village was nothing like she had expected. The lessons she'd received at the *Institute* painted a very different picture of the region. The morass, as the broader Middle East was now called, was supposed to be a barren and desolate wasteland populated by marauding tribes of criminals and terrorists. Yet, below her, nestled between rugged ridges was a thriving community of families living peacefully.

A tear traced a path down her cheek as she thought how much Henry would have loved it here. The Sakkin technician had longed to be part of a family, to be surrounded by people who loved and cared for each other. He'd given his life so that Wilda and the others could be free. That was a sacrifice she would never forget.

Leaving the outcrop she followed a ridgeline a little higher. The sun was on her back now, she could almost feel its healing powers flowing through her battered body.

She paused at the point where the ridge joined the bulk of the mountain. Here the goat track split. The path she usually took went right, dropping back down to the village. The other went left and wound its way higher. In the dozen times she'd walked the trail she'd never gone left. However, today something drew her in that direction, and she hobbled along the path as it wove between outcrops of granite.

As the climb got her blood pumping, the wound in her side throbbed. It gained intensity as she pressed on, savoring the pain. It reminded her that despite Sakkin's best efforts, she was still human.

She reached a steep ravine where the wind was howling, and realized she couldn't go any further. The trail descended steeply, impassable in her injured state. Frustrated, she turned and started back toward the village.

She took a few paces then paused as she heard something from the canyon. At first, she thought it was the howl of the wind rushing between boulders, but then it gained in intensity, the distraught wail of an animal in need.

Returning to the ravine she peered down into the rocks and bushes. The wailing noise continued, louder now, a forlorn cry from what she could only assume was a dog.

Throwing caution to the wind she started down the steep slope. Digging her walking stick into the gravel she used it as an anchor to control her descent. Halfway, she paused and listened.

A long drawn out howl confirmed that the dog was in a cluster of boulders a dozen feet below, surrounded by thick thorns. Sliding slowly she found a tunnel that animals had burrowed through the bushes. Thorns snagged her clothes, and her wounds sent pain shooting through her body as she crawled inside.

As she approached, the wail of the trapped animal intensified. The sound led her to a narrow gap in the rocks. Peering into the dark space she spotted the animal wedged between two boulders. It was a small dog with caramel-colored fur and black ears.

"Hey, it's going to be OK, little guy," she murmured as

she reached down and grabbed him by the scruff of his neck. He hung limp as she plucked him from the crevice and placed him on the ground.

She'd never seen a dog like this before. The animals that wandered the streets during training had all looked alike, long-legged and lean with pointy ears. This one was small and chunky with floppy black ears, a short snout and curled up tail. Creases on his forehead made him look like he was permanently frowning.

Wilda held her hand out the dog and he gave it a tentative sniff before licking her. "You're welcome," she said.

Feeling somewhat elated by her successful rescue mission Wilda crawled out of the bushes and made her way slowly up the slope. Stopping to let the pain subside she turned back and saw that the dog was following her. She waited as he scrambled up the hill and stood a few feet away, watching her.

In the soft morning light she could see grey around his muzzle and wisdom in his eyes.

"Going my way?" she asked.

He cocked his head sideways before scrabbling up the rocks to the trail above. There he sat and turned back as if to tell her he was waiting.

"Oh, it's going to be like that, is it?" She half expected the dog to stay with her for a short distance before returning to his home. He definitely wasn't from the village. Their dogs were like the ones in Syria. However, once she'd reached the mountain trail, he tagged along, seemingly content with her tortoise-like pace.

A half-hour later, as she emerged from the thorn bushes that bordered the shepherd's hut, she spotted Behdin sitting on a rock.

"Good morning. Father has invited you to join us for

breakfast," he said when she was closer. "Did you go for a walk?"

"Up the hill a little." She paused to catch her breath.

"Is it getting better?" he asked?

"Slowly."

The Kurdish teenager peered past her into the bushes. "Is that a dog?"

Wilda turned and saw that the little hound was standing at the edge of the thorn bushes. "I found him in the hills. If he follows me home, I can keep him, right?"

Behdin nodded. "As long as he doesn't chase the goats. He looks hungry. You should bring him to breakfast."

"He might tag along."

It was a short walk through the fields to Behdin's family home. Constructed from thick mud bricks, it had a flat roof made from a mixture of iron and solar panels. It was a cozy four-room residence where Behdin lived with his father, mother and sister Xeyal. They'd offered her one of their rooms, but she insisted on staying in the shepherd's hut. It would make leaving that little bit less painful if she could slip away in the night. Additionally, if Sakkin made their move before she was healed, they might grab her and spare the others.

As they approached, the rich smells of the breakfast that Behdin's mother, Serav, was cooking hit Wilda's nose, and her stomach growled.

"Was that the dog?" Behdin asked with a chuckle as he opened a wooden gate and waited for Wilda to enter. She stepped through and turned to see if the dog would follow. The small hound paused a half dozen feet from the wall.

"Come on then," he said.

The dog didn't move.

"I think he's happy there." Wilda followed Behdin

through the family's lush vegetable garden into the courtyard. In the summer months they usually cooked and ate their meals here, on a sturdy wooden table under a canopy of vines.

"Good morning!" Behdin's younger sister Xeyal jumped up from the table and launched herself at Wilda.

She braced herself, but the teenager hugged her gently.

"Are you feeling better?" asked the children's mother as they sat. Serav passed Wilda a plate of cold meat, boiled eggs and greens. Her husband, Haval, joined them at the table.

She smiled. "I'm getting there."

"Wilda found a little dog on her walk," said Behdin.

"A dog," exclaimed Xeyal. "Where is it?"

"He's outside the gate," he said. "I'll show you."

The curly-haired girl and her brother dashed from the table.

Haval shook his head. "Those two! Wilda, you should not go too far from the village. There are raiders and bandits in the hills."

"I'll be careful."

"Careful is not enough. Don't go into the hills alone." Like most of the villagers, Haval found it hard to comprehend their stories of Sakkin robots and airships. He assumed Behdin and Xeyal had been abducted by raiders.

"What are you doing today, dear?" Serav asked her husband, redirecting his attention.

"Working on the water purifier. The stream will dry up soon, and the bore water is salty."

"If you can't fix it, what will happen to my garden?"

"It will die, and we will starve."

Haval finished his breakfast and rose from the table as Behdin and Xeyal returned.

"He's so cute," the girl gushed.

"But he won't come closer," added her brother.

"Put some food out and give him some time," said their father as he kissed his wife on the cheek. "I will see you for lunch."

"Wilda, would you like to help me in the garden?" asked Serav, once her husband had left.

"Yes, I'd like that."

"Can we help too?" asked Xeyal.

"No." Her mother chuckled as she cleared the table. "The two of you need to go to school."

"That's so unfair," said Behdin. "How come Wilda doesn't have to go to school?"

"Because something tells me that Wilda has learned more than enough hard lessons for one lifetime."

Chapter Two

Los Angeles Enclave, North America

Manfred Lisker wasn't a man used to sitting in the wings. The CEO of a billion-dollar security firm, he was accustomed to being the most important person in the room. However, when it came to the Sumsunto corporation, he didn't rate a seat at the table. The six men and two women who surrounded the polished thousand-year-old Californian Redwood table were some of the most influential people on the planet. They controlled the resources, food and equipment that the isolated enclaves of the Advanced Block (ADBLOK) required to survive and thrive. There were other corporations, but Sumsunto was largest and, as such, was Sakkin Industries' most important client.

The meeting was one that occurred every financial quarter, and Lisker's presence was testament to the fact that his people were critical to Sumsunto's dominance of global manufacturing. Sakkin Industries provided security for the corporation's mining and agriculture activities outside of the safety of the ADBLOK. Over two-thirds of his workforce, trads, ganics and clankers, was committed to their largest client.

"That brings us to the next point," spoke the American at the head of the table. The eighty-year-old Sumsunto chairman looked barely middle-aged with smooth skin and piercing blue eyes. "Rare earth minerals."

From his chair at the rear of the room Lisker's ears pricked at the mention of the ultra-expensive commodity. REMs were the critical component in Sumsunto's manufacturing of fusion reactors, and underpinned their delivery of technology to the ADBLOK. He knew for a fact that the Chinese mines were nearing depletion. They needed to find a new supply, and that might come with additional opportunities for Sakkin.

Sumsunto's head of resource procurement took his cue from the chairman and began speaking, "Initial surveys indicate significant deposits of REM located in eastern Turkey and Northern Iraq."

"Kurdistan!" exclaimed another official. "You want to mine in the morass?"

Lisker suppressed a smile. The morass was the name given to the region formerly known as the Middle East. Devastated by conflict, it was a wildland of tribes, shattered cities and irradiated ruins, the perfect environment for Sakkin to capture a lucrative security contract.

"Yes," continued the resource chief. "Unless you know of a REM deposit somewhere else, perhaps here in California?" His sarcasm silenced the other man. "I'm seeking a budget to conduct further exploration."

The chairman nodded. "Manfred, is it really that bad?"

Lisker rose as he straightened his jacket. "The tribes and criminal elements in that region are well equipped and organized. They will pose a significant threat to any mining operations. However, Sakkin Industries have several assets in the area, including a forward operating base where we've been conducting operations to destabilize criminal elements."

"Would it take much for you to expand your operations?" asked the resource chief.

Lisker shrugged. "If we want to control the area, we need to ensure the tribes remain fractured. That will require additional resources."

"Go away and crunch your numbers and come back with a price," said the chairman. He turned to the resource chief. "How much do you need for initial scoping and planning?"

"That depends on—"

"A number, give me a damn number."

"Ah, thirty million."

"Approved." He rose from the table. "That concludes our business. Manfred, I appreciate you and your people making the trip." With that, one of the most powerful men on the planet departed the conference room, followed by three executive assistants.

The other attendees of the meeting followed suit, except for the resource chief who made a beeline for Manfred. "How long will it take you to develop a plan?"

He stood. "I'll have something to you within forty-eight hours."

"Excellent." The executive shot Manfred thumbs up before following the others out of the room.

Alone Manfred gazed out through the windows at the vast metropolis of Los Angeles. Once dominated by sprawling ghettos, traffic, and pollution, the enclave was now a vista of glass, water and greenery. The city of twenty million souls represented the apex of modern civilization. Since Sumsunto perfected miniature cold fusion in 2036, and led the push for California to secede from the United States, LA had emerged as a cutting-edge tech enclave.

Protected from the outside world by walls, drones and Sakkin security forces, inhabitants lived exceptionally long and healthy lives, oblivious to the suffering, fear and hate that were rife in the outside world. He liked to think of the populace below as sheep and Sakkin as the sheepdog that kept them safe. There were wolves beyond the green pastures, and it was their job to hunt them down and kill them.

Leaving the conference room he rode a high-speed elevator to the roof of Sumsunto tower, where his aircraft was waiting. The sleek grey vertjet was the fastest and most comfortable in the Sakkin fleet. The size of a medium business jet it had stubby wings that ended in ion thrusters. Autonomous and capable of vertical flight, like a helicopter, it covered the distance between LA and Sakkin's HQ in Cape Town in less than six hours.

The craft's side door was open, and he stepped into the luxury interior, handing his coat to a waiting assistant. Making his way aft, he joined two other men already seated in plush leather chairs.

Avi Lerner and Dominik Skarvin were dressed similarly to Manfred, expensive well-cut suits and crisp white shirts. Both, like him, were former intelligence officers who'd swapped their national loyalty for money and the luxuries that came with it.

"How did it go?" asked Avi Lerner, Sakkin's Head of Covert Operations, as his boss sat.

"Very well."

The aircraft trembled as Manfred fastened his seatbelt.

Silently it lifted into the air, turned slowly and accelerated. They climbed smoothly as the jet transitioned from vertical lift to forward flight, taking less than a minute to reach cruising altitude.

Manfred exhaled as he unfastened his belt. Takeoff in the vertjets always made him slightly uneasy. A stewardess appeared with a glass of his favorite single-malt whiskey on ice. He took the glass and sipped the golden liquid, savoring the burn as it slid down his throat. "How many men do we have in Kurdistan?" he asked Avi.

"At the Proteus facility?"

"Yes."

"Just the one operative, Yitzhak." Avi took his drink from the waiter, a gin and tonic. Dominik, Head of Operations, already had one in hand.

"Yitzhak Gorahn, I remember when that old dog was running Kurdish rebels into Iran. I can't believe he's still around."

"He joined us after Jericho," said Avi, referring to the nuclear detonation that had triggered the greater middle-eastern conflict and the destruction of Israel, Iran, Jordan, Lebanon and what remained of Syria.

"He knew the region, so I put him into Kurdistan in case we ever needed to operate there. He's been playing the tribes off against each other for over a decade now."

"Excellent foresight. Sumsunto has discovered rare earth minerals in the area. We need to develop a plan to secure both their exploration and future mining operations. I want to lead with clandestine activities before expanding into conventional security operations."

"We can leverage off Yitzhak's work and base out of the Proteus facility."

"Then we can increase our footprint with additional

ganics and mechops," added Dominik in his thick South African accent. "There is already a small contingent at that facility."

Lisker nodded. "I'll speak to Marnisha Copeland."

"Is she going to have a problem with this?" asked Avi.

"No, merely a formality. She's been running a new lab in Rwanda, the Kurdish facility is scheduled for closure." He took another sip of whiskey. "Does Lascar have a presence in the area?"

"Not that I'm aware of."

Dominik shook his head and snickered.

Avi shot him a dirty look.

Lascar was an organization that worked outside the ADBLOK. Officially they distributed humanitarian aid and supplies. From Lisker's point of view they were a criminal entity, and were known to support tribal terrorist elements. They were a thorn in Lisker's side that, so far, his head of clandestine operations had been unable to mitigate.

"This is a massive opportunity for us. Lascar, or anyone else, cannot be allowed to jeopardize it."

"Then I need additional resources to target them," said Avi.

Lisker's eyes narrowed. "If we can secure Sumsunto's rare earth supply, funding will not be a problem. You will both have what you need to destroy Lascar and anyone else who gets in our way."

Turkey-Kurdistan Border Region

The sniper made a slight adjustment to his scope, sharpening his view of the drone. The boxy craft hovered, its pulse engines stripping the ground below it of dust and debris.

"What is it doing?" asked his partner, laying alongside, peering through a pair of binoculars.

They were hidden on a rocky slope a short distance from where the car-sized autonomous aircraft was stationary above the valley floor.

"Masrour says it is checking for minerals."

"It can do that without landing?"

"It would seem so. Confirm range and windage."

"Five-hundred and twenty yards, wind running from two o'clock at three knots."

At that range the wind would have minimal impact on the twenty-millimeter ultra high-velocity projectile loaded into the breech of his weapon.

He exhaled slowly as he gently squeezed the trigger. The key to accuracy with a rifle this large was to not anticipate the violence that was about to be unleashed.

As the firing pin smashed into the primer the propellant ignited, accelerating a bullet larger than his finger to over four-thousand feet per second. He'd barely registered the brutal buck of the compensated recoil when his spotter reported a strike. Working the bolt he chambered another round and reacquired the target.

The drone wouldn't need another. His shot had hit the propulsion system, delivering sixty-thousand foot pounds of energy into the ion thrusters. It fell to the ground in a smoking and spluttering heap.

"Target destroyed," reported his spotter.

It took them less than thirty seconds to break down the heavy rifle and abandon their position. Making their way down the mountain they were met by a battered pickup.

"Good shooting," yelled the driver, through his open window.

The two men climbed into the bed and the truck took off along the valley floor in a cloud of dust. It skidded to a halt twenty yards from the downed drone.

The sniper grabbed an axe, slid from the bed and ran to the shattered body of the aircraft. With rapid blows, the hardened steel sliced through aluminum, carbon fiber and plastic revealing the innards of the million-dollar robot.

"You found it?" his spotter asked.

"This is it." He used the blade of the axe to pry a component the size of a handheld radio from its fixtures. Handing the axe to his partner, he wiggled a dozen cables from their sockets and pulled his prize free. "Let's go."

As the truck bounced along the valley floor he examined the cold metal box. There were characters engraved on the side, a nonsensical jumble of letters and numbers that would mean something to the technicians. He pondered the fact that something so small could be so valuable. Four separate teams had watched different valleys for the chance to a down a drone. Their commander, Masrour, had promised the successful team a reward of ten goats. The animals would go a long way to feeding his family of six.

He cradled the box the entire three-hour journey from the valley back to his hometown. Then, on the outskirts of town, he carried it deep into an abandoned mine, the stronghold of the Barzani militia.

"Well done, Razim," said his commander, Masrour as he took the device. "You have certainly earned your prize."

The sniper watched with interest as Masrour took the device to a man he had not seen before. Razim knew a warrior when he saw one, and the stranger may have been hunched over a computer, but he looked like a soldier. He peered over so he could see what was happening with the device.

"The computer is encrypted," said the man.

"Can we get in?" asked Masrour.

He shook his head. "No, but we can access the location data storage in the navigation system. That will tell you where the drone has been."

"Revealing the areas that could be targeted by mining operations."

"Correct."

The stranger tapped his fingers on a tablet as Masrour and Razim watched. A moment later he handed the commander the tablet. "They've been busy. This survey drone has covered most of your territory and the surrounding tribal areas. I've seen similar activity in a number of regions."

"What happens next?" asked Razim.

"They move their equipment in and poison your land."

"We will fight back."

"You can't do it alone," said the man.

"The Barzani does not need allies," snapped Masrour. "We need more weapons."

Village Of Pendro, Kurdistan

Wilda inhaled deeply as she burrowed her hands into the peaty soil of one of the raised garden beds. The earthy odor was comforting, but at the same time somewhat alien. Dust, blood, smoke and burning fuel were the scents that marked her childhood. Time in Serav's garden allowed her to escape from those memories.

Placing the seedling Serav had given her into a hole, she packed earth around it then lifted a watering can. There was a soft growl from behind as she poured. Turning, she saw that her new friend, the small brown dog, was facing the gate with his hackles raised.

"What's up?" she asked as she lowered the can.

The dog shot her a concerned look before fixing his attention back to the gate.

A moment later a figure appeared on the other side of the barrier. It belonged to Palin, whose mother was the tribal chief, and father the head of police. Tall with an athletic build and brooding good looks, he had shown a lot of interest in her since she'd arrived.

"Doing a little gardening?" he asked.

Wilda nodded as she reached for her walking stick.

He made to enter the garden but stopped when the dog growled. "Who's this little guy?"

"He doesn't have a name yet," said Wilda as she approached the dog. Ignoring the pain as she knelt, she offered the dog her hand and was rewarded with a sniff and a lick.

"He looks vicious," he said, sarcastically.

She gently placed a hand on the dog's head and stroked his soft black ears. "Looks can be deceiving."

"True." His eyes narrowed. "How are your wounds? You seem a lot more mobile."

"I'm good." Wilda gave the animal one last pat. "I've got a lot to plant, so I'm going to get back to it."

"So, no plans to move on?"

She rose and turned to face him. He met her gaze with crossed arms.

"Wilda, where are you?" The shout came from the village side of the garden. Xeyal appeared and stepped past

Palin, pushing open the gate. "Where's the dog?" she asked. "Is he still here?"

"I missed you too," responded Wilda, with a laugh.

Behdin wasn't far behind his sister and confronted Palin at the gate. "Why are you here?"

"I was checking on our guest."

"And?"

"She seems to be doing well. Behdin, Xeyal, good to see you. Please give my best to your parents. I'm sure I'll see them at tonight's meeting."

Wilda watched him walk away. "Tonight's meeting?" she asked Behdin as he joined them in the garden.

"There's a big feast. Other tribes have sent their chiefs to talk."

"About what?"

He shrugged. "We'll find out when we go."

"We?"

"Yes, everyone is invited."

"Wilda, you have to come," said Xeyal from where she was attempting to coax the dog out from behind a stack of firewood.

"I think it's better if I stay here with the dog."

"You should come," said Behdin. "You're part of our tribe now. The dog will be fine without you."

"He needs a name," said Xeyal. "We can't keep calling him dog."

Wilda didn't expect the feeling of belonging that swept over her as she limped across to where the girl was kneeling. She'd only experienced it once before, that she could remember. It had been when a broken old warrior had given her a name.

"I think we should call him Henry."

Chapter Three

Resdec Plantation, South America

A rivulet of sweat dropped from Leon Wilkens' nose and splashed onto the tablet he was holding. "Fuck this place," he muttered as he tipped the device, allowing it to drip into the leaf litter below.

The disgraced former Chief Instructor of Sakkin Industries' premier operative training facility sat in the overgrown ruins of a plantation home, deep within the jungles of the country formerly known as Venezuela. Reassigned following the escape of trainee Eight Two, Leon had been transferred to the backwater Resource Delivery Conglomerate (RESDEC) soy plantation, with orders to resolve a minor security problem. A problem that once he'd arrived, had turned out to be a borderline insurgency. A well-armed militia or RHE (Rival Hostile Element) had been attacking the autonomous clearing crews, destroying machinery, and slowing progress. However, in the next few minutes, all of that was going to end.

Turning his head he clamped his mouth onto the nozzle that protruded from the shoulder of his combat vest and sipped tepid water. In a climate-controlled berserker suit the water would have been ice cold, but Sakkin didn't allocate that level of equipment to a bottom-tier security operation. No, his arsenal was severely limited, consisting of four older model mechops, static security stations, a few drones, and monitoring sensors. Fortunately his two ganics, the nickname given to human operatives, were capable.

Wilkens spat warm water against a crumbling wall and suppressed the urge to snap his tablet in half. Less than a month ago he'd commanded one of Sakkin's aerostats, an army of elite operatives and two squads of the latest generation mechops. Now, because of Eight Two, he was drenched in sweat, getting mauled by mosquitos, and mopping up militants using obsolete kit and two half-trained operatives. Even the thought of Marnisha Copeland's bastard creation sent him into a rage. Trainee Eight Two had ruined his career, and he was going to destroy her even if it cost him what little he had left.

A soft ping in his earpiece alerted him to a sensor update. He zoomed in on the map and saw that one of his drones had spotted a figure crouched at the edge of the vegetation. A split second later its multi-spectral sensors identified another twenty targets deeper in the jungle.

"They've taken the bait," he transmitted over his short-range radio.

"Ready to engage," reported one of the ganics.

"Reserve also ready," added the other.

The stocky operative rose grasping his weapon and left the dilapidated building. Following a scratch trail through the jungle Wilkens moved into a hide he'd constructed earlier.

Inside the camouflaged outpost, on a tripod, sat a squat black grenade launcher. Wilkens crouched behind the weapon and activated the targeting computer that would arm and guide the string of deadly bombs, snaking their way into the weapon's breech.

Wilkens forgot all about the oppressive humidity as he grasped the weapon's handles, flicked off the safety and focused on the heads-up display.

His enemy was behaving exactly as he had predicted. The open ground beyond the camouflage netting that hid his position was a no-man's land of mud and splintered wood. Massive tracked harvesters had smashed the jungle into a pulp before loaders hauled it away to factories where it would be turned into furniture and clothing. In the coming days other machines would sow belts of hybrid soy to feed the ever-growing population of the ADBLOK megacities. Leon felt the slightest twinge of remorse as he aimed the grenade launcher toward the far edge of the trees where the militia was rallying. If he were one of them, he'd want to stop the destruction too. But he wasn't, and killing them was the only way he was going to get out of this shit hole. Plus, they were stupid enough to fall for his ruse and deserved to die.

He watched and waited as the ensemble of fighters massed in the cover of the jungle. Their target was a massive land clearing dozer seemingly stranded a mile into the cleared zone.

Glancing at his tablet he checked that machine remained where he'd positioned it. The feed from the overhead drone showed the maintenance crew was still working to repair the 'damaged' dozer. Given that there were only two of the autonomous land clearers working at the site, it had taken some convincing to allow the project boss to let him expose one as a come-on target. Offline for twenty-four hours, it cost millions for it to sit idle with a small security detail. On his tablet he could see two clankers positioned on either side of it. The older generation mechops weren't as capable as Sakkin's latest, but they helped set the scene.

The enemy was at the very edge of the jungle now and had formed themselves into a skirmish line. Wilkens rested his finger on the trigger and gently squeezed. "Engage!"

His grenade launcher barked, spitting a volley of bombs at the enemy. Simultaneously his two ganics opened fire from their hidden positions, lashing the forest with explosives and shrapnel.

"Ceasefire."

The gunfire and explosives may have fallen silent, but the crackle of flames and the screech of startled birds carried on the breeze. Wilkens turned his attention from the grenade launcher to his tablet, sending his Hunter drone in for a close look at his handiwork.

As the buzzing disc dropped from the sky, its thermal camera revealed the annihilation below. Sophisticated sensors outlined the victims beneath the jungle canopy, or what remained of them.

A smirk appeared on the Sakkin veteran's weathered face as he saw that his grenades had scattered pieces of the fighters over an area the size of a tennis court.

An icon appeared on his tablet and his smile faded. There was a second, smaller squad, located deeper in the jungle, beyond the reach of his grenade launcher. Having witnessed the slaughter, they were rapidly withdrawing.

"Crispy, mop up those squirters," he ordered.

"Yes, boss," snapped his senior ganic.

He watched as the teenager's indication icon tracked rapidly through the jungle on a path to intercept the fleeing rebels. Despite being wounded by Eight Two and expelled from Sakkin's operative program, the teenager was one of the most lethal ganics Wilkens had ever trained. Driven by rage he was an unstoppable juggernaut who responded instantly to every command.

Switching his tablet to a feed from the camera on Crispy's helmet, Wilkens watched as the ganic sprinted through the jungle. He caught a glimpse of a figure and nodded with satisfaction as a railer round blew it apart. The speed with which Crispy was moving made it difficult to see what was going on. Wilkens switched back to the overhead view from the drone and watched as the icons denoting the hostiles were marked as neutralized.

"Six targets eliminated," reported Crispy.

"Collect all of the weapons," he ordered as he used his tablet to summon an autonomous vehicle to his location.

"And the bodies?" Crispy asked.

"Leave them. The others might get the message," Wilkens replied as he began dismantling the grenade launcher.

"Director Glover would like to know if you're finished with his clearer?" the man's voice in his ear belonged to the personal assistant of his client, the RESDEC Site Manager.

"We've eliminated the threat. I no longer require its use."

There was a pause as the assistant relayed the message. "The Director would like to see you in his office."

"Of course he fucking does," he hissed under his breath as he detached the grenade launcher from its supporting tripod. "When?"

"As soon as possible."

"I'm on my way." He lugged the twenty-pound weapon out of the jungle as an electric utility vehicle approached.

The autonomous buggy came to a halt at the jungle edge, and he dropped the launcher into its cargo bed. Climbing into the passenger module he transmitted a message to his team. "Debriefing at the compound in thirty minutes."

Throwing his personnel railer on the seat opposite he closed the door and reveled in the air-conditioned comfort. The buggy accelerated across the freshly cleared landscape, its articulated suspension and powerful electric motors propelling it at forty miles an hour. It passed the massive clearer that was now powered up and prepared to go work slashing its way through the jungle.

When the buggy hit an access road it accelerated to seventy miles an hour. The view from the window changed from mud and shredded trees to fields of vibrant green soy plants. Acres of RESDEC crops flashed past as the buggy ripped along the access road, passing automated trucks hauling loads of beans to the central refinery.

Gazing out at the thousands of hectares of soy Wilkens couldn't help but feel disgusted at how far he'd fallen. The buggy slowed as it approached the walled compound that housed the RESDEC facilities and staff. It entered a security checkpoint where it stopped in a kill chamber covered by remote weapon turrets, bristling with railers. It took a moment for the scanners to clear the vehicle, and then blast doors opened. The buggy descended a ramp into the transport hangar, stopping in front of thick glass sliding doors.

"Have the cargo sent to my office," he ordered as he stepped out of the vehicle, unloaded his railer, and placed it in the back along with his assault vest.

Passing through the doors he strolled along a corridor to a bank of elevators. The facility's systems had already scanned his face and would give him access underground to his destination.

A baby-faced assistant shot him a look of disgust as he entered the manager's office. Wilkens paused in front of his desk, conscious that his camouflage fatigues were still damp with sweat. "Is there a problem?"

"No problem."

"I thought as much." Wilkens strode through another set of doors into Glover's private control room.

Brian Glover, a tall wisp of a man, stood over a three-dimensional map that allowed him to monitor every aspect of the massive RESDEC operation. "Leon, I believe congratulations are in order."

"The threat has been neutralized, for now."

Glover nodded as he used his hands to enlarge a portion of the map and review the productivity of the sector. "It will be important to maintain pressure on the terrorists."

"I have no intention of allowing them to recover from this. We will crush any sign of resistance." He paused. "However, we also need to go after the people supplying them with weapons."

Glover glanced up from the map. "You know who they are?"

"I have an inkling."

"And what are Sakkin Industries doing about it?"

Wilkens paused. "Not as much as they should."

Glover studied the operatives' grimy features. "I'm guessing you have a plan."

He stretched his neck. "I want to send one of my men to follow up a lead in the Middle East."

"Leaving us shorthanded."

"We've broken the back of the insurgency. Now is the time to strike against their support network. I can assure you that I have more than enough assets to target whatever remains."

Glover turned his attention back to the map, using his hands to enlarge a portion of the jungle. "I need another thousand hectares cleared by the end of the month. That will agitate the local riff-raff."

"Without weapons, they're not a threat."

"True. You may redeploy one of your men."

"Excellent. I'll keep you informed of our progress. Once my mission debriefing is complete, I will send you the report."

"Keep it brief. I don't have time for a novel."

"Is there anything else?"

Glover dismissed him with a wave of his hand, and Wilkens departed his office, ignoring the assistant on his way out.

It was a short trip via an electric cart to his isolated corner of the camp. His above-ground outpost consisted of several portable buildings clustered around a sizeable domed equipment shelter. Entering the structure he checked to see that the mechops were in their bays before making his way to the team room.

His two human operatives were seated at a central table running diagnostics on their equipment. The taller of the two, a broad-shouldered youth with intelligent eyes, spotted his boss and leaped to his feet.

"Take it easy, Tree, you'll give yourself an aneurism. We're not at the *Institute*." Wilkens slumped into a chair. "Crispy, what was the final count?"

His other operative stared at him through one functioning eye in a face that had been molten by a plasma grenade. Formerly known as trainee Seven Nine Nine, his injuries had earned him the nickname, Crispy. His offsider, trainee Three Three, was called Tree due to his physical presence.

"Thirty total KIA. Weapons recovered; Twenty-five assault rifles, eight rocket launchers and two recoilless rifles," Crispy croaked. The flame that had scorched his face had also damaged his voice box.

"A few thousand weapons more and Sakkin might reassign me to something less shit," said Wilkens.

As effective as his ganics were, according to Sakkin both were failed trainees; teenagers formerly part of Wilkens' training program at the *Institute*. Like him, their careers had been cut short by the traitor, a traitor who Wilkens was going to do everything in his power to destroy.

"Tree, run the clankers through a diagnostic, and make sure all the gear is stowed."

"Yes boss."

Both operatives rose, but Wilkens gestured for Crispy to remain. "I've got something else for you."

Tree exited the office with a questioning look on his face, leaving Wilkens alone with the disfigured ganic.

"I'm sending you to Turkey."

"What, why?"

"That's where that bitch Eight Two will have gone."

"How do you know that?"

"Because that's where—" he cut himself short. "Because that's where she was born. She'll try to go back to her village. I want you to find her and kill her."

The molten mess that was the right side of Crispy's face seemed to throb and his eye glowed with intensity. "When do I leave?"

Wilkens grabbed a tablet that was on the table. As he touched the device, it logged into his settings, displaying his calendar. A glance told him there was a Sakkin supply shuttle due. "You fly out tomorrow. Don't screw this up, Crispy. We're not going to get another chance."

Village Of Pendro, Kurdistan

"Come on, Wilda, we're going to miss the meeting." Xeyal took Wilda by the hand and dragged her toward the village.

The two of them had worked in the vegetable garden with the dog, Henry, till sunset. Then, they'd heard a bell ring summoning everyone to the square.

"I can't walk as fast as you." Wilda's side was hurting, but not as much as it had previously.

Xeyal slowed a little as the pair crossed a wooden bridge over a stream and arrived at the heart of their settlement.

The town square was an open area at the base of a steep hillside. Above it, homes were built into the rocky slope.

Most of the village had already gathered, sitting above the open space so they could see the activity below. Wilda saw that tables were arranged in a U shape with the village chief and elders seated at the head. She didn't recognize the other people sitting opposite. She assumed they were from different villages and tribes.

Xeyal spotted Behdin, sitting on a low wall, and they joined him.

"What are they saying?" asked Xeyal.

"They're discussing a defense pact to protect us from hostiles."

"Sakkin?" asked Wilda.

He shrugged. "Anyone who threatens the village. Some of the other villages have had livestock stolen and children kidnapped. They want us to join with them to defend the region. We're going to vote on turning the village police into a militia so we can deploy them."

"You really think a village militia could stand up to Sakkin?" Wilda asked quietly.

"We've done it before, haven't we? Bandits, raiders, Sakkin, whoever comes, we need to be able to protect ourselves. I think a unified defense is the best defense."

Wilda felt a pang of sadness at his words. The young man shouldn't have to concern himself with such matters. He should be focused on enjoying life and planning his future. As she watched the proceedings, she spotted a small group of men sitting off to one side, a short distance from the table. They were dressed in drab robes and had the look of professional warriors. Unlike the men of Pendro, and nearby villages, they were clean shaven.

"Who are they?" she asked Behdin.

"Barzani, they're a tribe from further south. They've been having meetings with the Chief, but Palin says they only came to spy on us. OK, the Chief is calling for a vote."

Wilda sat quietly as Palin's mother, the tribal chief, announced the terms of the vote. When they called for hands to be raised, Wilda abstained, but she saw that both teens voted in favor of raising a militia, along with most of the village.

She was torn as she watched the celebrations that followed. Part of her wanted so badly to join the villagers in their feasting and dancing. Another part feared that their pact would result in the village's youth being sent to their death against Sakkin mechops and drones.

"Wilda, I got you some food." Behdin's voice dragged her from her thoughts. He offered her a plate laden with fresh salads and grilled lamb.

"Will you and Xeyal join the militia?" she asked, taking the plate.

"Just me, girls aren't allowed to fight."

Her eyebrows raised.

"Although, they might make an exception for you."

"I'm not interested in fighting."

"What are you interested in?" he asked softly.

She shrugged and focused her attention on the food. "I'm not sure."

"Well, you're pretty good at gardening."

She let out a sigh. "Anything is better than combat."

"Tell that to Palin," he said, nodding to the crowd of people in the square. The chief's handsome son was reveling in the announcement that he was to command the militia.

"He's a just a silly boy who wants to play soldier. You've seen what mechops and ganics can do. Palin wouldn't last a minute out there."

"Maybe he just wants to keep his family safe." Behdin rose and made his way back to the crowd below.

As he walked away she realized he'd taken the comment personally. She rose to go after him, but pain shot up her side. Instead, she walked slowly back to the garden. She knew that the best thing she could do for Behdin and Xeyal was to heal and move on. Before Sakkin, finally caught up with her.

The dog was curled next to the gate that led out to the fields. They walked together back to the stone hut, where she sat on a flat rock. She gazed up at the sky, where stars were starting to appear. Out to the west, over the mountains, she could see the first glimmer of the Guardian Star. As she watched, it gained in intensity, stirring faint memories of a village and a beautiful woman with flowing brown hair and almond-shaped eyes.

She felt something on her leg and glanced down to see that Henry had placed his little muzzle on her thigh.

"It's OK, I'm not leaving just yet," she whispered as she stroked his ears.

Cape Town Enclave, Africa

Marnisha Copeland uncorked a bottle of Pinot Gris and poured it into two crystal glasses. Placing the bottle on her apartment's marble kitchen counter, she checked the digital display on her refrigerator. On the screen a small icon was tracking across the city of Cape Town toward her location.

Smoothing her figure-hugging silk dress she set off across the penthouse, her heels tapping on the mahogany wood floorboards. Her timing was impeccable. She opened her sliding glass doors at the exact moment the autonomous air taxi touched down on her private landing pad.

Avi Lerner stepped out of the craft as the doors opened. The wind whipped through her hair, and she immediately regretted wearing it down. It was always windy, forty stories above the city streets.

"Marnisha, you look ravishing as usual," said Avi as he stepped inside, and the doors shut behind him.

Tucking a strand of hair behind one of her ears, she smiled. "Beware the tall, dark stranger whose tongue is laced with sugar."

He laughed as he removed his suit jacket and she hung it by the door.

Like Manfred Lisker, Avi rarely wore anything other than the finest of suits. Marnisha couldn't remember seeing him in anything else unless you counted her bed linen. Despite their rivalry within Sakkin's hierarchy, the two had been on-again off-again lovers for decades. His muscular body was one she knew every inch of. Not just in the bedroom, but because she had personally repaired and enhanced it in the very earliest days of Sakkin's exploration into genetic modification and bionic enhancement.

She led him through the kitchen, where they picked up the wine, and into her luxurious lounge room. Relaxing on a plush settee Marnisha crossed her long legs and smiled. "So, I gather this is more than a carnal visit?"

"Straight to the point." He took a sip of wine. "You've got a facility on the Kurdish border associated with the Proteus project, I believe."

"That's correct, and I'm guessing that you want to use it as a base of operations to support Sumsunto's expansion in the area."

He frowned. "How do you know about that?"

She shot him a coy look over her glass.

"Manfred, you're still letting him bed you?"

Marnisha thought she detected the slightest trace of jealousy in his voice. "Avi, I don't have to fuck everyone I want information from." She winked. "Just you."

Smiling, he took a healthy slug from his glass. "Fair enough."

"Manfred mentioned that there was a significant opportunity in Kurdistan and wanted to know what tweaks could be made to our next class of ganics at *The Institute*."

"And?"

"They will meet the requirements of the company."

"Unlike your pet project." He snickered. "Wasn't that a cluster fuck."

Her eyes narrowed. "I do believe you had something you wanted to request."

"Less of a request and more of a heads up. Manfred has given me *Carte Blanche* on this project. Think of this as an act of courtesy. Your facility is critical to our plans. If you agree to hand it over to my division, I won't have to go through the formality of having him reassign it."

She took another sip from her glass, savoring the rich flavors. The lab and associated security outpost that Avi needed had been a critical part of the Proteus Project, a program aimed at providing Sakkin with genetically enhanced operatives. However, the technology within it was dated.

"I'm happy for you to use the facility. Although, there is a sensitive area that needs to continue functioning over the next few weeks. It will be completely off-limits to your people."

"Manfred told me the lab was being decommissioned?"

"Correct, however, there is a capability that I need to remain online until it can be replicated at the new lab."

"And that is?"

"Genetic data storage, nothing that would interest you."

His eyes narrowed. "Nothing to do with trainee Eight Two?"

She managed a grim smile. "No, pharmaceutical related. The rest of the facility is yours to do what you will. You can fill it with your robots, for all I care." Finishing her wine, she placed it on the table and stood. "Now, I've got a lot of work to do tonight." She slipped her shoulder from the sleek silk dress and shrugged out of the garment, letting it fall to the floor. "So, I'd appreciate it if we could cut to the sporting part of the evening."

Avi's eyes drank in the perfection of her elegant, albeit genetically modified body as she strode to her bedroom in nothing but her heels. He made a mental note to look into her 'genetic data' operation at the facility as he followed her, discarding his clothes. If there was one thing he knew about

Marnisha Copeland, it was that nothing was ever as it seemed.

Village Of Pendro, Kurdistan

Wilda always knew they would come. The only variable in her mind was how long it would take them to find her.

Their vertjets came in hard and fast, deploying mechops on all sides of the village so no one could escape.

Henry's bark had warned her, and she'd slipped out of bed and donned her jacket before the first craft had landed. Creeping out of the hut she glanced up at the night sky and caught a glimpse of the glow coming from an ion thruster as it swept overhead.

A feeling of dread descended upon her as she spotted a second and third aircraft. Henry growled as she heard the whirring blades of a drone. It was an entire strike force. The newly formed militia wouldn't stand a chance against a single Sakkin unit, let alone multiple mechop and ganic strike teams.

Ducking into the hut she fumbled for her cane and then shut the agitated dog inside. She set off in the direction of the first aircraft.

Tears welled in her eyes as she stumbled over the rocky ground. Everything she'd been through had been for nothing; Henry's death, the sacrifice of the refugees in the battle of Homs. People had died so that she could be free, and now that was over.

Something clanged to her right. She turned, expecting to see the hulking figure of a mechop. Her genetically-enhanced vision revealed one of the flocks of goats that Behdin's father grazed in the hills.

"Halt!" The electronic voice startled her as it bellowed in Kurdish.

"I'm the one you're looking for," she announced to the mechop that had appeared.

The machine paused, no doubt relaying her response to the commander of the mission. All the time, its weapons and sensors were aimed at her. It had been months since Wilda had faced one of the deadly machines. With its light absorbent skin, the eight-foot humanoid mechop looked far more sinister than she ever remembered.

"You will be detained," the machine announced in English.

She held her arms in front of her, and the mechop snapped carbon cuffs around her wrists, automatically drawing tight. Then the machine grasped her around the waist, slung her over its shoulder, turned and strode away.

Moments later she was dumped onto the ramp of a X22 Vertjet troop transporter. Lifting her head she looked directly into the molten features and hate-filled eye of Seven Nine Nine, the trainee who'd nearly killed her in the battle of Homs.

"You had to know we'd come," he hissed.

"Yes, and now you've got me. You can call off your dogs."

His mangled features split in a sickly grin. "Why would I do that? We haven't had our fun yet." He hauled her to her feet, dragging her inside the Sakkin aircraft. She recognized it as a command and control variant. Shoving her into a seat he attached her cuffs to the webbing base. "Wouldn't want you to miss the show."

Her vision was blocked as he jammed a VR headset

over her face. Suddenly, she was looking down at her village from what the Sakkin operatives called, God's view or eagle eye. A circle of blue icons showed that Sakkin units surrounded it.

"You've got me now. You don't have to do this," she screamed, struggling against her bonds. "They're innocent."

"Destroy the village. Exterminate them all," Seven Nine Nine ordered.

"NO!" She struggled against the cuffs as flashes of light appeared below her. The view displayed in her goggles switched to a camera mounted on one of mechops. A stream of super-heated plasma shot away from her, igniting a row of houses. Though the shimmering heat she spotted a figure as it burst into flames.

"NOOO!"

Thrashing her head back and forth she dislodged the goggles. Then, with a superhuman effort, she tore the straps on her chair and made for the aircraft's lowered ramp.

She stumbled from the vertjet and hit the ground. Rolling she came to a stop facing the village. The sky was red with fire as Sakkin operatives burned Pendro to the ground.

"Isn't that pretty," said Seven Nine Nine.

She turned back to where he was standing, clad in his exoskeleton armor, a smile on his sickly deformed face.

"I'm going to kill you," she hissed.

He laughed, lifted his arm and aimed the suit's railer at her. "You'll die long before me."

Wilda sat bolt upright in bed, her body drenched in sweat, heart racing. Lurching toward the door she pushed it open and stared through the darkness at the village. There was no fire in the sky, no mechops and no vertjets. Relief washed over her. Then, as quickly as it came, the relief was replaced with the harsh reminder that it was a sign of what would happen if she stayed.

Slumping to the ground, she buried her face in her folded arms. Ever since she escaped the *Institute*, death had followed. Scores of resistance fighters from Homs died battling the Sakkin forces attempting to hunt her down. Her friend Henry, the technician, perished defeating the Sakkin offensive. She would not let that happen to Xeyal, Behdin and the other villagers.

She looked up at the Guardian Star and her despair hardened to anger. Once a slave of Sakkin Industries, they had not only taken her childhood, but her future. She would make them pay for that.

She felt pressure on her leg and glanced down to see that the dog had placed his head on her thigh. Stroking his ears she turned her attention back to the Guardian Star, where it hung above a distant mountain range.

Chapter Four

Sakkin HQ, South African Zone

Seven Nine Nine stepped off the ramp of the vertjet that had transported him from South America. His scarred jaw dropped as he took in the setting before him. The shuttle bay was massive, at least twenty times the size of the one at the *Institute*. He glanced up the walls of the cavernous space at the aircraft that hung from hydraulic cradles. There had to be over a hundred vertjets of various models housed in the facility; enough aircraft to carry an army of mechops across the globe.

"Seven Nine Nine, you are to report immediately to Warehouse Echo to receive your consignment."

He glanced at the uniformed Sakkin officer who'd approached the landing pad. "How do I find that?"

The man pointed to the floor where a flashing green line had appeared. He followed it out of the hangar into the halls of Sakkin's headquarters. It led him past autonomous carts laden with equipment, and formations of clankers marching in step. Doors opened as he approached, and soon he was standing in a massive warehouse filled with racks of mechops. He stood in awe of the firepower contained within the single room. What's more, the designator Echo, told him there were at least another four, probably just like it.

With a soft whine a robotic arm appeared on a track that hung from the roof. It grasped a rack containing a half-dozen robots and lowered them to the ground.

The mechops were unlike any model he'd seen before. They were smaller, more humanoid and coated in some kind of light absorbent material. He noted that the previously visible sensors that adorned the robot's face were hidden. Where its face should have been was a smooth continuous surface.

"They're beautiful, aren't they?"

Crispy turned to find that a gentleman in a suit had entered the warehouse.

"Latest signature-reduction tech," said the man. He stepped around him and inspected the serial number on the closest clanker's chest. "Alpha Xray Eleven, adopt profile Kurdistan zero four."

The mechop's skin rippled as it changed color and shape. Crispy gasped as it morphed into something resembling an elderly bearded man dressed in faded brown robes.

"That's amazing."

"My own design," he added proudly.

"And you are?"

He smiled, flashing straight white teeth. Everything about the man seemed to be perfect, from his hair to his face, clothing and gleaming leather shoes. "My name is Avi Lerner. I'm the head of covert operations here at Sakkin."

Crispy swallowed. He was in the presence of greatness; they'd taught them about Avi Lerner at the *Institute*. The former Mossad officer had been there from the beginning. He was the right-hand man of Manfred Lisker, the chairman.

"And you are trainee Seven Nine Nine, or should I call you, Crispy?"

If his face hadn't been a mass of scar tissue, he would have blushed.

"You had the displeasure of dealing with trainee Eight Two?" Avi asked.

He nodded, fighting the urge to touch his mangled face.

"And Leon Wilkens has sent you to find and kill her, right?"

Crispy didn't say anything.

"Loyalty is an attribute I admire." He smiled. "Leon and I have a common goal here. I want her neutralized too. I also want you to know that you've got a friend in the silver tower." He gestured to the warehouse around him. "If you need anything, message me directly. Keep me across your mission, and when you succeed, I'll have you upgraded to full Operative." The Sakkin director smiled as he gripped Crispy's shoulder. "Oh, and we'll also fix up that face."

He watched as Avi Lerner strode out of the warehouse, and the doors shut behind him. This was a turn of events, he thought. Suddenly he had support for his mission at the highest levels of the company. Now it didn't seem so daunting. He was going to find Eight Two and tear her heart from her chest.

"Seven Nine Nine, you are to report to bay sixteen with your consignment," the robotic voice came from a hidden speaker, snapping him from his thoughts.

"Mechops, follow me."

He was filled with pride as he led the advanced robots back through the corridors to the designated landing bay. When he arrived, he noted that the aircraft waiting was a VX44, the big brother of the vertjet he'd flown in earlier. He waited as an automatic loader slid a pallet of human-sized canisters into the cargo bay. Wisps of fog clung to their metallic surface, telling him they were ice cold.

As he waited he glanced over at the adjacent bay and spotted a team of ganics boarding another jet. He'd never seen a craggier looking group of men. Half of them had bionic limbs, and their equipment looked like it had been through hell and back.

"Heavy hitters," said a Sakkin worker who'd appeared from inside the craft. "OK, you can load the mechops now."

"This aircraft is going to Turkey?" he asked.

The man glanced at his tablet. "That's correct, and it's due out in four minutes, so you better get your clankers on the damn thing."

On time, the craft trembled as its four thrusters fired up. It flew smoothly out of the hangar and rocketed skyward. From within the cargo hold, Crispy managed a wry smile. Things were looking up. Not only was he on a mission to kill his nemesis. Now he had a patron in the highest levels of Sakkin and that, he glanced at the rack of latest generation mechops, came with serious benefits.

Village Of Pendro, Kurdistan

Wilda was weeding a bed of heirloom tomatoes when the crack of a gunshot echoed off the cliffs to the west of the village. She recognized it was an AK47, an antique but capable weapon. Walking stiffly from the garden, with Henry at her heels, she almost collided with Behdin. The teen was heading in the direction of the gunfire with a Dragunov sniper rifle slung over his shoulder.

"Where did you get that?" she asked.

He shrugged. "I kept it."

When Wilda had arrived in the village, she'd been severely wounded. Waking from a fitful sleep, she'd learned that the village police had confiscated the weapons they'd brought with them from Homs.

Another shot rang out, and Wilda put out her hand for the gun.

Behdin shook his head. "Girls aren't allowed to join the militia."

"They're training?"

"Yes, do you want to go and watch?"

"Not particularly."

A burst of gunfire sounded from the valley, and Wilda fought the urge to run toward it.

"Come on. I know you want to."

She glanced down at Henry. "What do you think?"

The dog wagged his curled tail and let out a bark.

"See, he wants to go," said Behdin.

"Fine."

The gunshots increased in regularity as they made their way along a path toward the edge of the village. As they neared the cliffs she spotted a group of men sitting under a tree watching three others fire weapons at barrels thirty yards away.

Wilda and Henry sat with a group of children who were watching from a distance. Xeyal was among them, and she and the others rushed to Henry. Wilda smiled as the dog dutifully accepted the pats and cuddles. In a matter of days his temperament had changed from wild and skittish to something that bordered on affectionate.

The bark of an AK startled the group, and she glanced toward the shooters. Palin was standing at the makeshift firing point with a rifle tucked into his shoulder. She watched as he closed his eyes and jerked the trigger, sending a stream of bullets across the fields.

A cheer sounded from the men as a stray bullet slapped a drum some thirty yards distant.

She shook her head in disgust and rose to leave when she saw Behdin making his way to the firing point. As he approached, one of Palin's friends blocked his way. Her acute hearing caught the man's words. "This is a job for men. Leave the rifle and go and sit with the children."

Behdin made to step around the man, but Palin blocked him. "You heard him."

Wilda rose and walked stiffly toward the men. "Why don't you let him shoot? Or, are you afraid he's going to be better than you?"

Palin shot her a look of scorn. "You don't get a say here. This is men's business."

"Men!" She laughed. "You call yourself a man? I've seen better shooting from girls half your age."

Palin scowled. "You think you can do better?"

"You don't want to go there," said Behdin.

"Come on then. Show us." He thrust his AK into Wilda's hands.

She stood still as the cold metal of the weapon triggered memories that she'd been trying so hard to suppress. The screams from her dreams seemed to echo softly across the valley. She could almost smell the smoke and feel the heat of combat.

Palin turned to his comrades. "She's scared."

"Come on, Wilda. Show them," whispered Behdin.

Exhaling, she pushed the memories from her mind and let her training and instinct replace them. Calm confidence washed over her as she inspected the AK. In less than a second, she'd assessed it as being serviceable.

Stepping forward she cleared the weapon, shouldered it, snatched a magazine from atop a barrel, inserted it, chambered a round, and adopted a combat stance.

Time slowed as she aligned the metal sights onto a distant drum and pumped shot after shot into it. Emptying the magazine she took another and reloaded, before blasting the other targets. She unloaded the smoking AK and tossed it to a slack-jawed Palin. "Warriors are not limited to men and their egos."

Behdin let out a low whistle as Wilda turned her back on the men and returned to the children. "Come on, Henry. Let's get back to the garden." The little brown dog barked and followed.

She paused at the edge of the forest as a single shot rang out, followed by the clang of it striking a target. Turning, she saw that the men had let Behdin shoot. They were gathered around the boy as he fired and hit another distant target, all except Palin. The son of the village chief stood aside, watching her. She ignored him, returning to her walk back to the garden. As she made her way through the fields she noticed the pain in her flank had lessened. With any luck, she'd be able to depart the village in the next week or so. In the meantime, she had vegetables to tend. She'd leave the guns to Palin and Behdin.

Rwanda, Africa

"This was one of our first off-site facilities," said Manfred Lisker as his private vertjet descended smoothly. "I remember. Terrorists destroyed it." A bulkhead screen revealed the view of a camera mounted under the craft as it descended onto a concrete pad.

"Correct, it is now one of our most secure locations," replied Marnisha Copeland, the only other occupant of the aircraft. "The new facility is buried a hundred feet underground with a four-mile boundary patrolled by our latest drones and mechops. It's impenetrable."

They touched down gently and waited for the concrete pad to retract underground. When the aircraft had stopped moving, the side door opened, and they exited into a well-lit reception area. A uniformed Sakkin officer greeted them once they'd passed through an airlock.

"Chairman Lisker, welcome to the Lifebright Facility. Doctor Copeland, welcome back."

Marnisha acknowledged the man with a wave of her hand. "Hamish, I'll be showing the Chairman around."

He nodded and left them in a gleaming white hallway.

"He's one of three ganics here," she said, leading him deeper into the facility.

"The others?"

"His assistant and a security operative, everything else is automated."

"Impressive."

Doors opened as they approached, revealing an open workspace lit by a ceiling of luminescent panels. The vibrant lights illuminated production lines of medical machinery.

"What's this?" asked Lisker.

"The bionics lab. Wounded ganics are brought here for enhancement, robotic limbs, gene-splicing, anything needed to get them back in the fight."

"How many can you treat?"

"Thirty, depending on injuries. When the facility isn't servicing Sakkin's needs, we can use it to treat ADBLOK clients. There is a suite of luxury apartments, suitable for even the most exclusive client."

Lisker nodded. "You've thought of everything."

She took a tablet from a holder on the wall and examined the screen. "We've got a ganic on ice if you would like a demonstration."

"Why not."

She inputted a command on the tablet, and a red light on the opposite side of the lab flashed. The door below it slid open, and an enclosed patient transporter appeared. The coffin-shaped trolley slid alongside a surgical robot and transferred its patient sideways under a transparent dome.

Marnisha read from her tablet as they approached. "Four Six is a twenty-five-year-old male severely injured during an RHE attack on a client facility in Australia. An explosion destroyed both his legs and severely damaged his torso."

Manfred peered into the surgical chamber. "He's still alive?"

"Yes, he's in stasis."

To Lisker, the body inside the tube looked like a slab of meat. The operative's body was hairless, the skin pale and both legs were missing below the knee. Cables and tubes ran from its chest into the surgical robot. "How long ago did it happen?"

"Seventy-two hours."

"They heal fast."

"Part of the genetic coding."

"It's a pity you can't program them to regrow their limbs. It would save us a lot of time and money."

As he spoke, robotic arms went to work. Lasers sliced open one of the stumps as another robot delivered a pair of replacement bionic legs. Nerve endings were bared and then fused to the electronic versions hanging from the black carbon fiber limbs.

"This is amazing," said Lisker.

"This is nothing. I want to show you something else." She led him out of the surgical facility, through a series of security doors into an even larger space.

"The money maker," said Lisker as he took in the rows and rows of upright tubes that filled the room. "How many?"

"Two hundred."

"New technology?"

"I've worked out how to speed up the process. We can grow a clone in five months and accelerate its age in a little under three years."

"Ready for the *Institute*?"

She nodded. "Physically and mentally."

He drummed his fingers on one of the tubes. "Really, so you've cracked the instability issue? You're telling me we can grow reliable foot soldiers?"

"These new ganics will be much more than foot soldiers. This generation will be equally effective in clandestine roles, infiltration, manipulation. This is the future of our security operations."

"One step at a time. You've done well, Marnisha. When does it come online?"

"I've got to transfer the last of the data from the Proteus lab in Turkey. Once that is complete, we can flick the switch."

He slapped the acrylic tube. "Make it happen."

As they made their way back through long corridors to the aircraft hangar, he asked another question. "Do you have any updates on your pet project?"

"Not at the moment."

"So, she could be dead?"

"She's not dead," she replied as they climbed into the vertjet.

"It's a dangerous world out there, Marnisha. At the end of the day, she's a teenage girl, albeit a very capable one."

"You don't know the half of it," she murmured as she relaxed into a chair and fastened her seat belt.

Village Of Pendro, Kurdistan

"These tomatoes are almost ripe, Henry." Wilda turned the fruit gently, examining it for pests. She glanced at the dog. He was standing on his hind legs with his paws on the edge of the raised garden bed.

"You guys are quite the gardening team," said a voice.

She turned to find Palin standing at the gate. The dog jumped down from the garden and let out a low growl.

Palin raised his hands. "I'm not coming in. I just want to talk."

Wilda returned to examining the fruit. "About what?"

"Where did you learn to shoot like that? Is what Behdin

says true? Did you rescue him and the others from the prison?"

She frowned. Having been critically wounded when she first arrived, Wilda had limited knowledge of what the others had told the villagers. It was now becoming clear that Behdin had omitted that she was formerly part of the organization that had kidnapped the children in the first place.

"In my tribe, the men and women fought, side by side," she answered. "The people who took Behdin and Xeyal took from us as well."

"And what tribe is that?"

His question triggered a feeling of despair. She had no idea what her tribe was. All she had were the dreams of her mother and the Guardian Star. "It is small. You would not have heard of them."

"Try me."

"We are called *Simeon*." The name was one of the ten missing tribes of Israel, part of the history taught at the *Institute*.

"And everyone from this tribe fights like you?"

She turned to face him. "We did."

"Did?"

"We were attacked and… I think I might be the only one left."

"I'm sorry to hear that." He paused. "Who attacked you?"

"Robots, like the ones that took Behdin and Xeyal." It wasn't exactly a lie. Mechops had attacked her village. However, Palin didn't need to know that she'd been abducted and trained by Sakkin.

"What you did with my gun. Can you teach people to do that?"

She shook her head. "Women aren't allowed to join your militia."

Over Palin's shoulder, she saw his mother, the village chief, approaching. She'd met the statuesque woman with flowing grey hair once when she'd first arrived. Since then, she'd found Hervin to be reserved. Two men, her security detail, followed at a short distance.

"Palin, Wilda, good afternoon," said Hervin as she arrived.

"Good afternoon," Wilda replied pleasantly.

"Is my son bothering you?"

Palin rolled his eyes.

"Not at all," she replied.

Hervin placed a hand on the gate. "Do you mind if I come in?"

Palin and the two guards waited outside as the tribal chief entered the garden. "Serav mentioned you had been spending a lot of time in the garden. She says it has never looked better."

"I think that is a testament to her skill and patience as a teacher."

Hervin locked eyes with her. "You fit in well, but I think there is more you could be doing. Did Palin mention that we need help to train our militia?"

"He did. But, I was under the impression that only men could fight."

Hervin sat on the edge of one of the raised garden beds. "Wilda, you would not know this, but my mother was a lot like you. She was a warrior. A member of a militia who protected her people from Daesh."

"You must be very proud."

"Yes, but when she died, the future of her people died too. Our people lost most of our young women, and it took the next thirty years for our population to recover. That will not happen again. Not under my leadership."

Wilda had never thought of it like that. Sakkin treated every operative as an asset, a number. They didn't have to think about such things as generational planning. They simply took what they needed from tribes like this, placing little value on human life. "If you build your militia you will only invite violence into Pendro. It is peaceful here. The troubles are far away."

"True, Pendro is safe, for now. But, like I said, violence has beset us before and there are indications that it will return."

"What kind of indications?"

"The marauder attacks against our neighbors are increasing in intensity and regularity. There are reports of aircraft flying over the mountains and a village to our south was destroyed by a mysterious illness. Wilda, we need to prepare for the worst and we need your help to train our men to fight."

She paused to reflect on the elder's comments. "What happens when there are no more men to protect the women? What happens when the village has no one else to protect it?"

Hervin frowned. "Are you suggesting we train everyone?"

"If you want to survive, everyone has to be able to fight."

"If I agreed to provide basic training to everyone above the age of sixteen, would you help?"

She exhaled slowly, considering the offer.

Hervin reached out and placed a hand on her shoulder. "You have extraordinary gifts, Wilda. There is no shame in using them to help people."

Wilda locked eyes with Palin, who nodded. While her injuries were preventing her from traveling, they would not stop her from providing basic training to the militia. What's more, it might help alleviate the suspicions of many of the tribe members.

"OK, I'll help, but only if Behdin works with me."

Palin scowled.

Hervin rose. "Thank you. Now, I have a meeting with the shepherds I must attend." As she passed through the garden, she inspected one of the plants. "I'll have them deliver some manure."

She passed her son at the gate and disappeared with her security detail.

"I am the commander of the militia," said Palin, when she was gone.

"Of course." Wilda returned to tending her plants. "I will be helping with training, that is all."

When he'd left, Wilda sat on the ground, leaned against the garden bed and sighed. The last thing she wanted was to tie herself to the village. She could kick herself for picking up the AK and showing up Palin and his group. Sensing her anguish, Henry moved closer. She tussled his ears and kissed the top of his head. "Why is everything so difficult?" she murmured.

Bismarck Facility, Eastern Turkey

Seven Nine Nine's flight to Sakkin's remote facility in the mountains of Eastern Turkey had been uneventful. The vertjet had touched down on the roof of a massive concrete fortress and deposited its cargo before departing on its return leg.

The view from the top of the concrete battlements was like nothing he'd ever seen. Ragged mountains stretched to the horizon in every direction. The wind howled between the weapons and sensors that adorned the structure. He felt like he was on the furthest corner of the planet, as far from civilization as you could get.

He heard footsteps from behind, and turned to see a figure approaching from an elevator. The man was old and gnarled as the trees that he imagined grew in this forsaken place.

"With a face like that, you must be Crispy." His voice sounded like gravel tumbling in a barrel. "That asshole Leon sent me an HF message telling me you were coming. I'm Yitzhak."

"I'm operative Seven Nine—"

"Cut the shit, kid. Just because Sakkin gave you a number, doesn't mean you have to be one. You've earned a real name. Wear it with pride. Now, get those fancy clankers stowed and meet me in the ops room."

There was no thought of answering back as he snapped into action. The mechops were standing to one side of the landing zone. He ordered them to report to the armory and followed them as they marched inside.

He noted that Yitzhak's equipment holdings were limited. There were only three older style berserker suits and a half dozen outdated mechops. The addition of the updated models had tripled the facility's combat power.

The operations room was located a short distance from the armory and the loading dock. Crispy was already enrolled in its access protocols, and the door slid open to reveal a standard Sakkin layout. The walls were covered in screens, displaying data from drones, ground sensors, weapon stations and remote cameras. A row of desks, usually occupied by staffers, was empty with touch screens blank and headsets long since discarded.

"You run this alone?" he asked.

Yitzhak grunted from the central terminal. "See anyone else?" An antique-looking combat vest and railer hung from the back of his chair.

"Not a lot going on here?" he asked, crossing the room to stand in front of a screen that detailed incident occurrences at the facility. It was almost empty, only containing a few reports of sheepherders bumping the outer perimeter.

Yitzhak laughed. "Kid, you've got no idea. Have a look at this." The Sakkin veteran tapped his touch screen, dimming the room's lights and activating a high-resolution holographic projector. Thousands of points linked by a spiderweb of lines filled the room. "Each of those points represents a tribe or family in this region. They've got a history of rallying together to face off against their enemies." He inputted more commands, and several lines turned red. "These are the relationships I'm working to sever or degrade to keep the fuckers splintered. Fighting each other instead of coming after us."

"How do you do that?" asked Crispy.

Yitzhak scowled as if to suggest the solution was obvious. "What the hell are they teaching you lids? I'm running agents who report to me on what's going on. I feed them information and resources to shape the decision-makers, generate a little friction where it's needed." He killed the holograph, and the lights brightened.

Crispy gestured to one of the monitors that showed the status of at least a dozen sensors. "You've got a lot of drones out. Is that to verify the intel they give you?"

"Now you're getting it."

"And that's why the security footprint is light." Crispy turned his attention to another panel that showed a 3D map of the facility. He touched the dashboard, activating a live feed from a camera deep in the facility. On-screen, figures in full protective suits were wheeling the cryogenic tubes that had arrived on his flight through a security door. He checked the available feeds for the area beyond the barrier. There were none. "So, what exactly happens here?"

"Bio shit, well beyond your classification and your understanding. Our job is to keep it safe and prepare for expanded operations in the region. What's more, I've got intel that local tribal elements have formed a defense pact. They've had their eyes on this place for a while. If they can amass enough combat power, they may even have a crack."

"They'd attack a fortress?"

He nodded. "The people in this area have a proud heritage of kicking ass. They fucked up the Turkish army, Iraqi army, and ISIS, you've heard of ISIS?"

"Of course, the Islamic State death cult. They seized control of most of Syria and Iraq in 2016."

"Yeah, well, they didn't last long in this area, and neither will we if we don't stay on top of things."

"What do you need me to do?"

"We're ramping up security for a drilling team they're sending in. I'll need you babysitting them. Don't let your hunt for the escaped trainee get in the way of my mission."

"Leon told you about that?"

"Of course. Although, fuck knows why she'd come out here. There's nothing in those hills but misery. I've added her to our watch list. If she pops up, I'll let you know, and if it fits into our operations, we'll put her down. Now, get yourself a room and something to eat. I'll run you through a full system brief in an hour."

As Crispy left the operations room and made his way to the accommodation and galley, he adjusted his journey to take him past the doors where the cry-tubes had disappeared. He paused for a second, trying to steal a glimpse of what was inside. He wondered if what was behind those doors was the reason Leon was so sure she would come to Turkey.

Chapter Five

Village Of Pendro, Kurdistan

Palin had to physically bite his tongue to stop from interjecting as Wilda outlined her intention for training the militia. She'd had his men lay out all their weapons and equipment and, having inspected the motley collection, had decided that they would start with weapon safety and maintenance.

It irked Palin that he had to take the advice of a teenage girl on what was men's business. Sure, his mother was the village chief, but it was his father who coordinated the village police, and now he commanded the militia. Women had no place in the village's security, especially a teenage girl and an outsider.

"So, we'll work through each weapon, covering the basics. Then we can move on to marksmanship and tactics."

Palin snickered. "We already know how to use weapons. My mother wants you to train a militia, not a shooting club."

"A weapon that fails to fire can be more lethal than one that does," she replied.

"How do you mean?" asked one of the twelve men gathered for training.

"Behdin, come and work as my cover man." She took a battered G36 assault rifle from the row of weapons. "Imagine that we are assaulting an enemy position. Behdin is covering me as I prepare to advance."

The teenager crouched next to a barrel, aiming his rifle at the imaginary threat.

"However, as I'm moving, exposed." She walked forward slowly. "A threat appears and is ready to shoot at me." She froze. "Behdin moves to engage, but his weapon jams. Now I am exposed and the hostile shoots. I'm dead."

"A little melodramatic. Surely, you could shoot the enemy yourself," suggested Palin.

"You couldn't hit a barrel when you were stationary. What makes you think that you could hit it on the move?" she responded, cheerfully.

Behdin laughed, but Palin silenced him with a glare.

"This makes sense," said the villager who'd asked the original question. "We should get started."

Wilda spent the next four hours with the twelve men, teaching them how to use and maintain each of the weapons. Then while they were having lunch, the chief joined them.

"Palin, how is the training progressing?" she asked.

"Good, we're going through the basics," he replied confidently. "After lunch, we are moving on to tactics."

She nodded, turning to Wilda. "Are the men performing?"

"Yes, they're doing well."

"Good. Palin, tomorrow morning the militia will

provide an hour of training to the entire village. Work with Wilda and decide what everyone needs to know. Plan for one session per week."

"That's not enough," said Wilda.

The Kurdish woman held up her hand. "It is enough. Any more and people will panic, and our food production will suffer."

Wilda bit her tongue.

"The militia is our priority," the chief continued. "It will meet our obligation to the mutual defense pact." She turned to Wilda. "Focus on giving them the best training you can."

Once the chief had departed, Wilda sat on the grass and patted Henry. "They don't trust me," she said as Behdin joined them.

"Who, the Chief and Palin? They don't trust anyone. That's why they're our leaders. If they trusted everyone, we'd always get the worst deal."

Wilda took a sip of water. "Let's get the training done so I can get back to the garden."

Village Of Harkanass, Kurdistan

The four-person security outpost was perched at the top of a valley where a narrow road crossed a high pass. Behind it, protected by steep cliffs, were the fertile lands that the tribe depended on for their crops and livestock.

Harkanass was an outlying settlement in the loose federation of tribes that made up the Kurdish region. Its people were proud and resilient, having survived decades of conflict.

"How long do you think we have until the first frost?"

one of them, a farmer, asked. All four men were wrapped in blankets to ward off the fresh evening air. The sun was setting behind a distant mountain, and soon it would be dark.

"Next week. You have plenty of time to pick your cucumbers," responded one of the others, a tall shepherd whose goat herd was not impacted by morning frost.

"We should light the fire," said the youngest of the group. The teenager was a technician, responsible for keeping the village's limited solar power systems running.

"Yes, put some tea on," added the fourth man who was sitting behind the checkpoint's fifty-caliber machine gun. Older than the others, he was the village judge. No one was exempt from security responsibilities.

As the farmer rose, all four men heard a sound like a cracking whip over their heads.

"We're under attack!" bellowed the judge.

More cracks sounded along with an explosion against the sand-filled barrels that surrounded the outpost. The noise was deafening as dust and smoke filled the air.

The tech hugged the earth, clutching his modified AK with a look of utter terror on his face.

"Watch the flanks! Watch the flanks!" yelled the judge between firing bursts from his heavy machine gun.

The shepherd and farmer heard his cry, grabbed their weapons, and headed for firing bays on either side of the post.

"Call the village," screamed the judge.

The tech nodded and franticly scrambled to the radio set that connected the outpost to their village five miles away. Clutching the handset, he screamed into it, "We're under attack. Send help. Send help!" A high explosive round burst above the position, shaking the roof and showering him in debris. "Send help. Send help." Another round hit the building, and he realized that the antenna was destroyed.

The heavy machine gun thudded to a halt. "More ammo," yelled the judge.

The tech grabbed two tins from a rack and lugged them to the gun.

"They're coming from the right. Go and help Sabal," the older man ordered as he deftly reloaded the heavy machine gun.

The tech found Sabal, the shepherd, hunkered on the western side of the outpost, clutching his assault rifle.

"They're coming along the ridgeline," said Sabal without looking away.

"How many?"

"At least ten."

He peeked through a gap in the sandbags and spotted figures among the rocks. Bullets clanged on the barriers as he aimed his rifle and squeezed off several shots.

"We're going to be overrun!" yelled Sabal.

The thought terrified the technician. Marauders were savages, and they would show no mercy. He'd seen images of bodies hung headless from trees and light poles. A bullet slapped into a sandbag mere inches from his head as he fumbled a magazine change.

"They're coming!" screamed Sabal.

He aimed his weapon through the firing slot and saw figures rushing the position. Pulling the trigger he sent a stream of bullets blasting toward them. The gun ran dry as Sabal grabbed his arm.

"We need to pull back."

He nodded, reloading his rifle as Sabal covered his move

back inside the outpost, where the judge was hammering with the heavy machine gun.

He'd reached the sandbagged doorway when he was hit. It felt like someone had smashed a sledgehammer into his shoulder and kicked him to the floor. Groaning he turned and saw marauders climbing the wall, not five yards distant. Time slowed as he saw the face of the man who would kill him. The long shadows cast a horrendous mask over the marauder's features and struck fear deep into his soul. Staring into the gaping maw of the muzzle of the attacker's weapon, he waited for the flash of flame that would end his life.

It never came.

Sabal cut the Turkish marauder down with a blast from his weapon then dragged the technician away. "Keep firing or we're all dead," he screamed.

The tech managed to prop his AK against his knee as he sat covering the entrance. Adrenalin was keeping the pain in his shoulder at bay, but he knew that wouldn't last long. Firing shots through the entrance he came to terms with the fact he was going to die.

Behind him, the fifty-caliber fell silent as the judge ran out of ammunition.

Spurred on by the lack of resistance, the intensity of the attack against the eastern side increased. He spotted figures through the gaps in the barrels as the marauders moved in for the kill.

"This is it," screamed the judge. "Make them pay in blood." It was the last order he would give. A bullet caught him as he moved to one of the firing ports, and he fell to the ground, dead.

Sabal's weapon chattered, and the tech fired two more shots as he felt the effect of blood loss. He could barely lift the AK. Frowning, he faintly registered a pop above him. Suddenly a brilliant white light shone down from the sky.

"It's the angel of God," he whispered.

For a split second the battlefield fell silent as all eyes looked skyward. Then, all hell broke loose.

Weapons barked, diesel engines roared, and men screamed.

"Stay with us!" yelled Sabal over the cacophony. "The cavalry has arrived."

Bismarck Facility, Eastern Turkey

Crispy heard the Sumsunto heavy transporter long before he saw it. Throbbing plasma engines echoed across the valley as it dropped out of the sky directly overhead the facility. He braced himself for the onslaught of the downdraft as it hovered a dozen feet off the deck, blasting him with thrust. Then, with a thump, it touched down, and the engines subsided to a low whine as the ramp lowered.

A tall figure clad in fluorescent orange workwear strode down and made a beeline for Crispy, extending his hand.

"Hey, I'm Brad, team leader of Bramos crew."

"My name is Seven… Crispy, you can call me Crispy." He shook the man's hand. "How many in your crew?"

"Just me, a few tin heads and the rig." He gestured over his shoulder at a small truck that was descending the ramp.

The vehicle was about the same size as the electric utility vehicles they'd used in Venezuela. Instead of seating and a flat bed, it was laden with equipment. As it descended and stopped in front of the cargo elevator doors, he noted two robots attached to the rear, Brad's tin heads. He walked over and inspected the clunky-looking robots. They resembled stripped-down clankers, nothing like the sleek units that he'd delivered from Sakkin HQ. "Small team."

"We travel light, but we get it done. Now, where can we stow our gear?"

"The system can park up in the garage. The head of security has asked that you join us in the operations room."

"Very well."

He led the Sumsunto employee into the ops room, where Yitzhak was waiting. Crispy noted it had been sanitized. The monitors only showed security camera feeds, and the primary wall display was a map of the area.

Yitzhak greeted the engineer before providing him a chair. "I've uploaded your proposed exploration sites." Green icons appeared on the map. "All but one is readily accessible by vehicle." He gestured to a location high on the side of a mountain. "We may need to coordinate air support for this."

Brad shrugged. "If we can get close, the tin heads can hump the gear. What's the situation regarding hostiles?"

"Bandits and marauders. Crispy will be running your security detail. We've got the latest generation of clankers. As long as you don't run into an army, we'll be fine. You got a tablet?"

He fished in the cargo pockets of his pants and pulled out a battered device.

Yitzhak took it from him and laid it on a transfer pad. "I'll upload a full briefing. You can go through it in your own time. We've allocated you a suite in the east wing." He returned the device as the ops room door hissed open, and a service robot appeared. "The clanker will show you where it is. We'll join you in the mess hall at 1800. Get yourself comfortable and we'll have a drink over dinner."

"Will do. Looking forward to working with you."

Once the engineer had departed, and the door was secure, Yitzhak reactivated classified feeds. "So, in the last twenty-four hours, marauders hit the northern checkpoint at Harkanass. The villagers rallied and managed to defeat them."

"Is that bad?"

"It is. The village is part of a loose defense pact that has been expanding in the region. Another village has agreed to send their militia to reinforce, should the marauders return. If they're successful, they will entice other tribes and villages to join the pact."

"Which might threaten our operations," Crispy said.

"The Barzani could be considering joining the pact. If that happens, they may be able to convince some of its members to target this facility, or worse Sumsunto's sites as they come online. We need to take action to ensure the tribes remain splintered."

"How do we do that?"

Yitzhak smiled. "We make sure their first little venture is an utter failure."

Village Of Pendro, Kurdistan

"There's one in that tree." Jorin, one of Palin's closest friends, gestured with his single barrel shotgun. "A big one."

Palin squinted as he searched the trees that lined the river for a partridge. "I can't see it." Shooting the fat little birds was one of his favorite past times. At least once a week he rose early to hunt them.

"Up there, next to the dead branch."

Palin shook his head and looked again. The early morning sun cast long shadows that played tricks on your mind. You had to focus on spotting a part of the bird that was easy to recognize. He usually identified the partridge's plump round body.

"See it?" Jorin asked.

"No."

"Out from the big fork on that middle tree. Not sure if it's a chukar, but it is definitely a bird. You want me to shoot it?"

"No, I don't want you to shoot it," he hissed. "Now shut up, before you scare it." Finally, he spotted the animal. Jorin was right. It wasn't a chukar. It was some other pigeon-looking bird. As he aimed his shotgun it rotated its head toward him. It looked odd, its eyes glassy.

The shotgun roared, spitting pellets into the tree. The bird fell like a rock into the reeds that bordered the river.

"Wow, if only you could shoot an assault rifle like that," said his friend.

"Just find the bird," he snapped. He sat on the bank, smoking a cigarette as Jorin searched the reeds. Half his cigarette had disappeared before his friend called out.

"Palin, you're going to want to see this," Jorin called from among the reeds.

"Yes, that's why you're in there getting it."

His friend crashed out of the reeds holding the creature by a broken wing. "This is something different. This bird isn't real."

Palin dropped his cigarette on the ground and crushed it with his boot. "What are you talking about?"

Jorin laid the bird on the bank. "It's not real. It's some kind of robot."

Palin knelt and inspected it. Jorin was right. From a

distance the bird had looked normal, less the clunky movement, but up close, it was clearly not organic. He poked it with the barrel of his shotgun, revealing circuitry and wiring. "Holy shit." Grabbing it by a wing he lifted it from the ground. It managed a flutter before he stuffed it into his satchel. "I'm taking this to my mother. Don't mention it to anyone."

Jorin nodded.

"I'll see you at training."

Palin hurried back to the village to his mother's house at the base of the mountain. As he approached he saw a man on an electric motorbike heading out of town. Judging from his clothes, he guessed the rider was from one of the villages to the west.

He burst into the house and found his parents seated in the kitchen. "Who was that?" he asked.

"A messenger from Harkanass. How did your hunt go?" his mother replied.

The rider was momentarily forgotten as he hefted his satchel onto the table. "I found something strange." He pulled the bird from the bag.

"Palin, how many times have I told you not to bring game into—" she stopped mid-sentence as she noticed the bird wasn't real. "What is it?"

"I think it's some kind of spy device."

"A drone?" his father asked, poking the machine with his finger.

"Yes, and I think it's here because of Wilda."

"You don't trust the girl, even with the training she's providing?" His mother picked up the bird and scrutinized it.

"She knows too much about warfare. No one would teach a teenage girl that much."

"Different people do different things," said his mother as she placed the drone back on the table. "In saying that, her skills and the presence of a drone are things to consider. We will need to keep a very close eye on her."

"I can do that," added Palin.

She shook her head. "No, I've got a far more important mission for you and your men."

Sakkin HQ, South African Zone

Manfred Lisker swept into the Sakkin boardroom and took his place at the head of the polished marble table.

Sakkin's team of directors were already present; Andrew Dunbar, Head of Intelligence, Dominik Skarvin, Head of Operations, Avi Lerner, Head of Covert Operations, and Marnisha Copeland, Head of Bio Technology.

"Dom, update me on Turkey," he demanded.

"Yes, sir," Skarvin replied. "We've commenced forward staging of assets to the former US base in Incirlik. Sumsunto has deployed a survey team. We're ahead of schedule."

"Excellent." He turned to his right-hand man, Avi Lerner, Head of Covert Ops. "And your advanced activities?"

"Yitzhak Gorahn has been running a tight ship. Dunbar can vouch for his understanding of the tribal networks and their interactions. He's been playing them off against each other for years. I'm confident that he can facilitate exploration as required."

"And there is no sign of Lascar influence in the region?"

It was Dunbar's turn to talk. "That's correct. Their

influence only seems to extend as far as Mosul. We haven't seen anything to indicate they have a presence in the Kurdish tribal lands."

"Is that something we should expect?" asked Marnisha Copeland. "If Sumsunto expands their operations in the area, may Lascar do the same?"

"Good question," added Lisker.

Dunbar shrugged. "Hard to say. It depends on what sort of impact Sumsunto's operations have on the tribes. In South America, they bulldozed tribal lands. If their mining is more discreet, it may not elicit an uprising."

Skarvin laughed. "Sumsunto does nothing discretely. They will flatten entire mountain ranges, burn forests and raze villages. With our latest generation of mechops and ganics guarding them, there will be nothing Lascar or anyone else can do to stop them. Our operations in Venezuela are proof that Avi's soft-touch approach is an unnecessary risk. Leon Wilkens has utterly decimated the RHE there with a handful of outdated clankers. We put him in charge of operations in Turkey, and he will eradicate any resistance.

"You don't know if there will be any resistance," said Avi. "You send an animal like Wilkens into the mix and you're likely to fuck everything up. Yitzhak has the situation well in hand. Keep your toys in Incirlik. If we need to drop the hammer, it's a short jump to Semdinli."

Skarvin chuckled. "If? It's only a matter of time. Your cloak and dagger bullshit never works. They're about as effective as Marnisha's science projects."

"Quit the squabbling," snapped Lisker. "The Kurdish venture is now the company's main effort. However, we cannot afford any degradation in other sectors. That includes our long-term goal of destroying Lascar. Marnisha, perhaps you could give an update on your projects?"

"My pleasure. As you're all aware, I've been working on enhancing our organic operative program."

"Because that worked out so well last time," interjected Skarvin.

"I've dialed back the independence to acceptable tolerances. We've learned a lot from Eight Two."

"Except, the location of that particular model," added Skarvin.

A look from Lisker silenced him.

"The most important discovery we've made is a reverse of the genetic engineering that has allowed us to slow the aging process. By manipulating the appropriate genes, we've been able to speed up the development cycle of our next generation of operatives."

"Does that have any side effects?" asked Dunbar.

She shook her head. "Not that impact us. The average working life of a ganic is six years. The enhanced and accelerated models will be capable of achieving ten, possibly more."

"What's the per-unit cost?" asked Lerner.

"A little over fifteen million."

"That's almost double the cost of one of my enhanced mechops," he said.

"Which are very impressive, but you still rely heavily on ganics, and most of your non-modified personnel are well past their use by date. This program will ensure the continued delivery of high-quality operatives into the future."

"Which is why it is fully funded," added Lisker. "Now, if there isn't anything else, I need to prepare for a briefing to the CEO of Sumsunto." He gave each of the directors a confirmatory glance then left the room.

Dunbar and Skarvin followed him out, leaving Lerner and Copeland. "When will the first batch of your super ganics be ready?" Avi asked.

"Three years."

"In the meantime, is there room in your budget for keeping my more reliable operatives functioning?"

"Avi, I've got an entire facility dedicated to just that. Talk to my assistant and schedule them in."

The handsome former Mossad operative smiled. "For a scientist, you seem to have a far more strategic outlook than any of us." Then he followed the others out of the room.

Marnisha sat gazing out through the wall-to-ceiling windows at the bustling Cape Town enclave. What she hadn't revealed to the others was that Eight Two was likely on a head-on collision with the venture in Turkey. There was a part of her that wanted to warn them. But there was also a part that wanted to sit back and watch the destruction.

Chapter Six

Eastern Turkey

Crispy guided the electric Combat Patrol Vehicle along the route designated by the buggy's heads-up display. He slowed as the cliffs on either side squeezed in on the narrow track.

The CPV was a staple in the Sakkin arsenal. Lightweight and powered by fuel cells, it was fast, agile and capable of operating for weeks without refueling. With its run-flat honeycomb cell tires and high clearance, it was ideal for navigating the narrow tracks that passed for roads in Semdinli.

Climbing over a pass and descending toward a stream Crispy eased off the power and slowed to a walk. Swiping a gloved hand over the windshield he replaced the navigation menu for a drone feed.

Nearly a mile in front of him a pizza box-sized fan drone flew over his destination. On-screen, he could see two trucks parked in a clearing alongside the river, his rendezvous point. Target designation software had identified six gunmen at the RV.

Accelerating he forded the stream and scrambled up the far bank. As he followed the track to the RV, he checked his rear camera to ensure that his cargo was still following. The CPV behind him operated in autonomous mode and was fully laden with equipment cases.

Three hundred yards from the RV, out of sight around a corner, Crispy halted. "Alpha, establish an overwatch position in this location." He placed an icon on the touch screen.

Behind him, one of the covert mechops alighted from the vehicle and selected a long-range railer from the weapon rack. He'd only brought one of the clankers. Three others were guarding the drilling team.

He watched as it strode off the road and paused. Its smooth skin shimmered, and it morphed into something resembling a cloak-wearing shepherd. Then, as it climbed, its clothes adapted to the rock around it, and it blended seamlessly, disappearing.

The icon on his map, which denoted Alpha, climbed rapidly. He waited till it was just short of the position he'd selected before driving forward. Rounding the corner he saw the men and trucks that the drone had identified. Four men stood in a semi-circle. Two hid in the rocks above.

Stopping a hundred yards short he stepped out of the CPV and adjusted his equipment. He'd opted to travel light, omitting an exoskeleton in favor of covert body armor and a penetrator pistol. The compact handgun fired ultra-high velocity exploding sabot projectiles that would blast through any of the protection the marauders wore. Over his armor he wore a battered olive-green jacket that matched his worn cargo pants and boots.

As he approached the men, he assessed them as high risk. They wore a mixed assortment of military uniforms and equipment with a broad range of weaponry. Yitzhak had briefed him on the marauders. They were criminals and terrorists who murdered, stole and pillaged to make their way in the world. Crispy didn't have a problem with any of that. He had an issue with how unpredictable it made them.

"Where are the guns?" asked one of the men in grating Turkish.

Crispy assessed him as their leader, Hamdi. He was a brute of a man with a shaved head and a fierce beard. His bulging arms made the M240 machine gun he was cradling look like a water pistol.

"I have them here." He gestured to the CPV laden with the cargo. "Yitzhak wanted me to confirm you understood the mission before I hand them over."

Hamdi's eyes narrowed. "Damn, you're an ugly fucker. Did you lose a fight with a flame thrower?"

"The mission, do you understand what is expected of you?"

"Fuck you. I could kill you right now and take everything."

"Incorrect," snapped Crispy. "Alpha, warning shot."

The railer slug was traveling at almost three miles a second when it hit a boulder next to one of the hidden men. Fragments of rock and dust exploded into the air as the magnetically-accelerated dart delivered its kinetic energy.

The marauders dove for cover, leaving Crispy standing with his arms crossed. "Your mission," he stated matter of fact, "Is to destroy the northern checkpoint at Harkanass and eliminate the village militia. If you do that, we will provide more equipment and weapons."

Leaving his weapon on the ground, the leader rose to his feet. "Sakkin cowards, always hiding behind your tech."

Crispy sighed. "Pick one of your men. Your best fighter."

Hamdi looked confused. "What?"

"I'll fight one of your men. One on one. Then we'll know who's weak."

The Turk smirked. "Ali, fight the ugly bastard."

One of the men handed his weapon to an associate and removed his combat vest.

Crispy took off his jacket and tossed it on the ground. Removing his pistol from its holster he placed it in the jacket.

His opponent looked to be slightly heavier and a little shorter. His stance told Crispy that he had a preference for wrestling and ground fighting. Taking that into consideration, he adjusted his feet and waited for the attack he knew would come.

Ali let out a roar as he rushed forward, hands low and ready to wrap up his opponent. The Sakkin operative moved with lighting speed, sidestepping and delivering a sharp jab to the man's nose.

Ali barely reacted to the stream of blood and tears. With his vision impaired, Crispy found it even easier to evade his next attempt to grab him. Once again, his punch found purchase on the marauder's face, however this time he followed it up with a sidekick that knocked his opponent to the ground.

"We done messing around?" Crispy snarled. "If you understand your mission, I've got your equipment. Mule, move to my location."

The cargo carrying CPV moved smoothly toward him, stopping a few paces away. Crispy grabbed one of the bulky cases and hefted it to the ground. Opening it he revealed the assault rifles contained within. "There's also mortars, grenade launchers, rocket launchers, everything you need to destroy that checkpoint. Then, when you're done, I'll deliver the solar generator and water purifier you wanted."

"And the radios?" asked Hamdi.

Crispy gestured to the crates. "They're in there somewhere. Get your people to unload this so I can get out of here." He tipped his head in the direction of the wrestler, who remained dazed, laying on the dirt. "Or maybe you've got someone else I can kick the shit out of?"

Hamdi let out a braying laugh. "I like this guy." He took one of the weapons out of the crate, locked open the breech, and inspected it. "We'll crush them. But when we do, I want one of the guns that splits rocks."

Crispy shrugged. "I'll see what I can do."

Village Of Pendro, Kurdistan

Wilda grasped a tendril from a tomato plant and gently wound it around a piece of wire. Tending the garden had become cathartic for her. Every morning she'd wake, take a short walk with Henry, eat breakfast, and then escape to her green leafy haven. She'd stay there until Behdin would collect her for militia training.

"Wilda, Wilda?"

She heard Behdin's cries a moment before he appeared breathless at the garden gate. "What? It's too early for training."

"The militia is loading up. Palin is taking them to Harkanass."

"The militia? They're not ready." She tucked the tomato frond away and stormed to the gate. In the last few days she'd finally recovered enough to walk freely without her cane. Breaking into a run she ignored the sharp pain in her flank and headed for the center of the village.

There were three trucks parked in the courtyard where Palin was supervising the loading of supplies and men. She made a beeline for the Chief's house and spotted her talking to someone in front of the building.

"Hervin, what's going on?"

The Chief excused herself from the conversation and turned to face her. "Wilda, how are you feeling today?"

She was caught slightly off guard by the question. "I'm doing well, thank you Hervin." She glanced back to the town center. "Why is the militia loading into trucks? Where are they going?"

"Walk with me, Wilda." The Chief turned and strolled through the village. "You are aware that we have a common defense pact with Harkanass?"

"They were attacked?"

"Yes, and they have requested our support. Palin will be taking the militia to reinforce their defenses."

"They're not ready."

"Neither were the villagers of Harkanass."

The comment struck home. "I should go with them."

Hervin shook her head. "No, that's not in the best interest of you or the village. Your wounds still need time to heal."

Wilda rolled her eyes. "None of these men have the experience I have. If they're up against anything serious, then you're sending them to their deaths."

"The marauders are nothing special. The village was

able to defeat them. The deployment of our militia is more of a message of support. I do not expect them to fight."

"Then why can I not go with them? Isn't it better to be prepared than sorry?"

"Wilda, the reputation of the village is at stake. I cannot send a teenage girl as a part of our militia. You are far more valuable as a trainer than a warrior."

Her almond-shaped eyes narrowed. "So that's it. Women can lead the village, but they can't fight to protect it."

"If the village were under attack, I would expect everyone to fight. This is different. It is not just about survival, it is also political. One day you will understand."

"I'm not a child, Hervin. I have seen more than most."

"I know."

Wilda turned and walked away from the Chief. As she passed through the square she locked eyes with Palin. There was something on the cocky militia leaders' face that she'd not seen before, uncertainty. They both knew that he and his men were not ready for whatever was waiting for them. Then, in a split second, the look was gone, replaced by smug suspicion.

Wilda had calmed by the time she returned to the garden where Xeyal and Behdin were waiting with Henry. "Are you going with them?" asked Behdin. "Palin said I have to stay and continue training everyone else."

"I need you both to look after Henry," she said.

"You're going with them?" Xeyal sounded ready to cry.

"Just to keep an eye on things. I'll be back in a few days, but you can't tell anyone I've gone."

"You're sneaking off?" Behdin asked.

"Hervin doesn't want me to go. She doesn't trust me. Just promise me you'll look after Henry?" She bent and ruffled the dog's ears. Then she rose and hugged each of them. "I'll be back soon."

Fighting her own emotions she strode across the field to the shepherd's cottage. Inside, she stuffed what few personal items she had into a small backpack. She'd been preparing herself to leave eventually, but not like this. Sitting on the bed she exhaled slowly. Something told her that she wasn't going to be returning. Wiping tears from her eyes she put on her jacket, gripped her backpack tightly and stepped outside.

"Wilda!"

She spotted Behdin running across the field toward her. As he approached he swung a black backpack from his shoulder. "You'll need this." He passed it to her.

The bag was hefty. Wilda lowered it to the ground.

"There's food, water, a pistol, grenades and ammunition," he said. "Not much, but it's all I have."

"Behdin, I can't take this."

"You have to Wilda. I need to know that you've got a chance." There were tears in the teenager's eyes.

She stepped forward and wrapped her arms around him. "You and Xeyal are the only family I have."

"Don't forget us," he whispered. "Come back to us safe."

The distant roar of a truck's engine snapped her into action. "I've got to go." She quickly stuffed the contents of her own small pack into Behdin's, slung it over her shoulders and started toward the road. Pushing everything from her mind but the mission she jogged to the corner of the field and vaulted a low stone wall. A twinge in her flank reminded her she wasn't fully healed.

A few hundred yards distant, the road from the village crossed a stream next to a collapsed bridge. It was the perfect spot to catch the trucks. Pushing through a thicket she caught sight of the convoy as it rumbled past.

She waited for the last vehicle to slow as it approached the stream then sprung from the bushes and sprinted after it. Grasping the tailgate she made to climb in. Before she could, hands grasped her jacket and rucksack, dragging her inside. Safely in the truck, she thanked the two members of the militia who'd helped her.

"We didn't think you were coming," said one.

"I'm not supposed to be here. Palin cannot know."

The men nodded.

"We wanted you to come. None of us have fought before. Palin said you needed to remain to train more men, should we need them."

She reached across and placed a hand on the scared young man's shoulder. "I couldn't let you have all the fun."

Chapter Seven

Turkey-Kurdistan Border Region

Crispy watched from a distance as the drilling rig used a pulse laser to cut through hundreds of yards of rock. The equipment made a god-awful sound that echoed off the valley walls and grated on his soul. Sometimes enhanced hearing was more of a curse than a gift.

A glance at the flexible tablet attached to his wrist told him that his sentries and drones had not detected anyone within five miles of their location. He sent an encrypted situation report to Yitzhak via the radio stack in his CPV. Then he checked the operations log for any alerts regarding Eight Two. There were none.

The drill ceased its high-pitched whine, and he saw that Brad had removed his hearing protection and was sitting on a crate inspecting his own tablet. Crispy strode across and stood a short distance away. "Have you found anything?"

Brad nodded as he fished in his pocket for a chocolate bar. "A shit ton of rare earth. This place is riddled with it."

"Good news for Sumsunto."

"Yeah, bad news for the locals."

"What do you mean?"

Brad offered him half of his chocolate. "Nothing, bro. Like you said, good news for Sumsunto. We need to refill the water supply for the cooling system. According to the map, there's a river at the bottom of this valley."

"I'll need to reposition my assets."

"Yeah, let me know when you're good to go."

Crispy interrogated his own digital map and saw that the two mechops armed with railers wouldn't have to move far to continue providing overwatch. He sent them on their way and tasked a drone to quickly surveil the river for possible threats. "We're all clear. I'll lead the way."

He steered the CPV along a narrow trail, checking his rear-facing camera to ensure that Brad was following. Derelict buildings dotted the landscape, and he weaved between them before coming to a halt alongside a fast-moving stream.

"This will do nicely," said Brad. He ordered his two robot workers to run out a water line.

Crispy watched as they hooked it to the truck, and Brad activated the pump.

"This'll only take a few minutes. Then we can head over to drill site three four."

Crispy wandered down to the water's edge and scanned the far side of the river. Among the wild shrubs and bushes he spotted what looked to be the remains of a settlement. A quick check of the feed from his drone confirmed that there were more buildings between the vegetation.

"Can't blame them for moving," said Brad, from behind. "This water is toxic. It's full of radiation, mercury, lead, all the good shit."

"It looks so clean."

"Yeah, no algae is gonna grow in that."

He glanced upstream. "Where's it coming from?"

Brad laughed. "Bud, it's flowing out of that concrete fortress you call Bismarck. I don't know what you're building in that joint, but it ain't healthy." His tablet pinged. "Tanks are full. We can hit the road when you're ready."

Crispy walked back to the vehicles with him. "So, if you drank it, you'd die?"

Brad shook his head. "Not right away. It would make you very sick, but it would take months to kill you. Wouldn't be a nice way to go."

"Good way to clear the locals out."

Brad paused. "Yeah, I guess. Once they start mining, all the water in the area's going to be stuffed anyway." Then he climbed into his truck. "I try not to think about that sort of thing. Right, only eight more sites, and we're done."

Northwestern Kurdistan

For young men, scared to death on their first mission, it hadn't taken Wilda's traveling companions long to fall asleep in the back of the truck. Usually, she could do the same. They had trained her to conserve energy at the *Institute*, but she had far too much on her mind.

She knew that, no matter what the outcome of this expedition, she was unlikely to ever see Behdin, Xeyal and Henry again. If she returned to the village, she was condemning them to death. Eventually, Sakkin would come for her and they would kill everyone.

Pushing the thoughts from her mind, she focused on the

possibilities of the mission ahead. She was working off limited information. From what Behdin and Hervin had revealed, the village of Harkanass had been attacked by marauders. They had taken casualties but had managed to repel the attack. Her training told her the likelihood of them attacking again was low, especially if they'd suffered losses. Marauders, brigands, whatever the name, they all had one thing in common. They only attacked weaker prey, and Harkanass had proven to have teeth.

She opened the ruck that Behdin had given her and inspected the contents. There was a pistol inside, a Glock, old but reliable. He'd packed three spare magazines, two high explosive grenades, an assortment of dried food, and a flask of water. It was a long way from what she'd carried at the *Institute*.

It seemed like yesterday that she was dropping into combat in a berserker suit armed to the teeth with railers, plasma grenades and augmented strength; a one-woman army descending from the sky to lay waste to the enemies of Sakkin.

So much had changed since then. She'd betrayed Sakkin, and lost her only friend, Henry the technician. She'd led a mass escape from a Sakkin death center, found a family, and now, abandoned them. Tears ran down her cheeks as she loaded the pistol and tucked it into her belt. She placed the other magazines and the two grenades in the pockets of her jacket. Just because she wasn't expecting the marauders to attack didn't mean she couldn't be prepared for the worst.

Out of the back of the truck she could see mountains on either side of the road. The valley floor was wider here with more farms and crops. It was dusk, and warm light escaped from the windows of homes that dotted the landscape. She imagined families sitting down together for their evening meal, sharing stories and enjoying each other's company. Then she imagined what would happen if a Sakkin strike team swept through the area.

The truck downshifted and slowed as they entered a village, Harkanass. People on the footpaths stared, and their scared eyes followed the convoy. It was another ten minutes of driving before they reached their destination.

Wilda jumped from the back of the truck and looked around. They had stopped at what looked to be a security outpost. Her genetically modified eyes revealed details in the moonlight; barrels, concrete blocks and sandbags were pockmarked with bullet holes and scorched by explosions. This must be the site where the marauders had attacked, she thought.

She hung back as Palin and his men gathered under a floodlight. Introductions were made to the local militia commander.

Wilda's acute hearing detected the whistle of the mortar bomb before anyone else. "Take cover!" she screamed, dropping to the ground.

The high explosive projectile detonated behind them alongside one of the trucks, flipping it onto its side and igniting its fuel tank in a massive ball of fire. The heat washed over Wilda as she lay flat on the dirt.

"Holy shit!" yelled the man next to her.

"Get inside," she ordered.

The men took up her cry, repeating the order and scrambling for the opening to the bunker.

More explosives rained down as the men piled inside, and the local militia rushed to their weapon ports. Wilda was the last in. As she entered, she came face to face with a panicked Palin.

"What are you doing here?"

The bunker shuddered as a round landed closer.

"They're going to blow this place to pieces," yelled Wilda. "We need to get out there and find the mortar team."

Palin stared at her blankly and then flinched as bullets thudded into the walls and cracked overhead. His men were hunkered down in the dugouts that lined the fighting position. To a man, they looked utterly terrified. "I'm going to need a rifle."

The young commander shook his head. "You shouldn't even be here."

Wilda glared at him before turning and sprinting out of the bunker. She dashed past the burning truck and out of the mortar's immediate impact zone. Sliding into a ditch she drew her pistol and gathered herself.

It took her a moment to locate the direction from which the enemy was attacking. That's where the mortar would be. If she stayed low and used the boulders for cover, she could get close to it and use her two grenades.

She ran wide around the security outpost. It was being lashed with small arms fire and high explosives. Moving fast, she relied on her enhanced vision to find every fold in the rugged terrain. It took her precious minutes to work her way along the flank until she'd reached the attacker's forward positions. Hunkering behind a rock a short distance from where a machine gun was firing, she glanced back at the outpost. There was limited return fire. If she didn't intervene, the attackers would assault, and Palin and the others would be overrun.

She checked the pistol was loaded and gripped it tightly. The last thing she wanted to do was take lives, to be what

Sakkin had trained her to be, a killer, but it was the only way she could save her friends.

Exhaling, she surrendered to the training.

The three men working the machine gun didn't stand a chance. Wilda shot them all in the head before moving through the darkness toward the mortar position. She was on the hunt now, nothing was going to stop her.

The marauder boss realized something was wrong when the first machine gun fell silent, and he couldn't raise them on the radio. He sent a pair of his men over to check, and a moment later, he couldn't contact them either. "Increase your rate of fire," he ordered the mortar team, before issuing another command over his radio. "Ali, commence the assault."

Back in the outpost, the Harkanass militia commander had managed to rally his men. Palin and his men, terrified of the mortars, remained hunkered under any overhead protection they could find.

"They're coming from the east!" screamed one of the Harkanass men as the intensity of explosions and bullets increased.

The militia leader, a burly local policeman, grabbed Palin by the jacket and dragged him toward the eastern side of the outpost. "Get your men on the wall, or we're all going to die."

While Palin struggled to lead his militia, Wilda was stalking her prey. She'd located the mortar team. They were positioned a short distance along a ridgeline, beside the track the marauders must have used to infiltrate. She spotted a group of parked trucks and pickups. Her keen eyes also identified two sentries guarding the vehicles. She stole through the darkness, behind them and slipped between the trucks.

There was a flash from the location of the mortar as it spat another bomb skyward. Taking a grenade from her pocket she wriggled the pin free. She gripped the handle tightly as she snuck toward the mortar. Finally, she was close enough to see the mortar team. Three men were crewing the deadly weapon. Two were ferrying bombs from a trailer as a third was listening to a radio and making adjustments to the tube.

She tossed the grenade in the trailer as one of the men spotted her, and all hell broke loose. Bullets ripped through the air around her as she sprinted back toward the trucks.

Diving to the ground she covered her ears and opened her mouth. Bullets slashed over her hitting the trucks, but there was no explosion. Her side throbbed and heart pounded as she realized how exposed she was.

Scrambling along the ground she made a few more yards before the grenade detonated. The small thud was immediately followed by a massive explosion as the mortar bombs detonated. The blast swept over Wilda and peppered the vehicles with shrapnel. Earth and rocks rained down like hail as she covered her head with her hands. A baseball-sized rock hit her square on the top of the head, stunning her.

Marauders and defenders alike stopped still as the massive explosion lit up the valley and echoed off the mountains.

"What the hell was that?" asked Palin, from below the parapet of the fighting position.

"I think the mortars just blew up," replied one of his men.

"She did it," he whispered. "She actually did it." He peeked over the edge of the sandbagged wall and saw flashes five hundred yards further along the ridgeline.

"Here they come!" someone screamed.

Bullets slammed into the sandbags around Palin, and he fought the urge to cower behind them. Aiming his AK to the east, he fired a burst before ducking into cover. Rounds snapped through the air where his head had been.

Wilda stumbled to her feet. She felt like she was back in the *Institute*, having fought a round with her former classmate Tree. The hulking trainee had shattered her jaw with a roundhouse kick that could have killed her. This felt worse. She touched the lump on her head and struggled to her feet. It took her a moment to realize she was still among the enemy, and another moment to locate her pistol.

She was a short distance from a marauder's vehicle and remembered that there had been at least two sentries. Her head throbbed as she made her way toward the trucks. Movement caught her eye, and she spotted one of the men crouched next to a technical. As she got closer she could see he was tending his friend, who'd been wounded in the blast. Aiming her pistol she began to squeeze the trigger. Her Sakkin training told her to show no mercy, but that wasn't who she was. The man was helping his friend, no longer a threat. Lowering her pistol she backed away and slipped into the rugged terrain that she'd used to infiltrate.

Gunfire from the east revealed the marauder's attack was still going strong. Shaking off her concussion she backtracked to where she'd annihilated the machine gun team and found an assault rifle and spare magazines. For a moment, she stood staring at the men she'd shot, a feeling of disgust welling inside. These men were killers, but even killers had families.

A burst of gunfire and the dull thud of a grenade reminded her of the task at hand. She cocked the rifle as she skirted boulders and bushes in a hunt for the attacking marauders. Pausing, she waited for the muzzle flash of their weapons to reveal them. They were less than a hundred yards from the security outpost and progressing steadily. Return fire from the outpost had waned. They must have been running low on ammunition. The marauders, on the other hand, seemed to have a limitless supply.

She identified a cluster of men moving forward and yanked the pin from her final grenade. Letting the handle pop, she held it for a few seconds and then tossed it high. It detonated above the men lashing them with shrapnel. She followed up with a burst from her rifle, hitting another two men and scattering others. Firing off the magazine she reloaded and doubled back toward the security outpost.

Looping around the way she had come she headed back to the burning truck. Pausing, she listened. The gunfire had trickled off to sporadic shots. The attack had been defeated. She let her rifle drop and sat alongside it. Tears streamed down her face and she gazed out into the night sky. No matter how hard she tried, she couldn't escape what Sakkin had made her.

Over a mountain, she spotted the Guardian Star. It was the only connection she had with her life before Sakkin. It was in every dream she'd ever had. She knew what she had to do.

Her backpack was where she had dropped it when they'd arrived, a short distance from the burning truck. Turning her back on the security checkpoint, she shouldered the bag and set off along the road. She'd covered a few hundred yards before she aligned herself with the star and started climbing the mountain.

Wilda had walked through the night and now sat on the side of a steep slope facing east as the glow of dawn rose over a distant mountain. She shivered as the first rays of sunlight hit her face. Her battered jacket had done little to warm her as the temperature dropped overnight.

The morning sun lit up the valley before her like a spotlight, revealing the treacherous terrain she had yet to cover. The further into the mountains she went the more rugged the ground seemed to become. Thankfully it also meant fewer settlements to avoid. The last thing she wanted was to run into marauders or another militia.

She took a paper bag of dried fruit from her backpack and chewed on a slice of apricot as the morning sun rose. Behdin's supplies weren't going to last long and she had no idea how far she had to travel. Water was her priority; her flask was nearly empty.

Her shivering subsided as the sun warmed her. Yawning she considered the idea of curling up in its rays and taking a quick nap to replenish her energy. The ache in her side had subsided, but her head was still sore from the mortar blast. Sipping her water she decided against sleep, opting instead to descend to the valley floor in search of water. Returning her things to the pack she shouldered it and began the climb down.

As she weaved her way through rocks and outcrops covered in thick brush, her mind turned to her dreams. The only link to her past, they were the key to finding out what happened to her mother and locating her village. She'd sketched the memories that came to her as she slept, but her notebook was long gone. All she had now was what she could remember. Her most recent dream had featured a concrete fortress in the mountains where her mother had been taken. The only other detail she knew was that it was under the Guardian Star.

As she neared the base of the slope Wilda spotted buildings among the vegetation on the banks of a river. Ducking behind a boulder she listened for any sign of human activity. Peering through a bush at the closest building, she noticed vines were growing through its collapsed walls. The village was deserted.

Wilda ducked under a sagging beam and stood in the entrance of an abandoned residence. All the windows were missing, and part of the ceiling had collapsed. Weeds had taken over what was once a large family home. She imagined that at some stage, not that long ago, the building had been a hive of activity. Now, not even animals called it home.

Exploring a little further, she looked for clues as to why the villagers had moved on. There were no signs of conflict. None of the debris left behind by war. No bullet holes, craters or spent casings. It looked as if the settlement's population had simply picked up and left.

On the outskirts of the small village were dry, barren fields divided by canals. The inhabitants had been farmers. Perhaps disease had wiped out their crops, she mused. As she made her way to the river she spotted what looked like diggings atop a low mound. Angling toward it she quickly realized it was a graveyard.

She counted fifteen dry mounds of dirt that looked like they had been dug about the time the village had been abandoned. Scanning the hills on either side of the valley she wondered what could have caused so many deaths. Had a virus wiped out the villagers and caused the survivors to abandon their homes?

Sadness swept over her as she imagined the fear and

misery disease would have brought. It took her back to her training and file footage she'd seen from the pandemic of 2027. However, this outbreak was far more recent. Perhaps the virus was back. With the enhancements that Sakkin had made to her immune system, it wasn't something that could directly impact her health. Still, it could be deadly for Behdin, Xeyal and the others.

Leaving the graves she made her way to the edge of the river and took her flask from her pack. As she stood on the bank she was amazed by the clarity of the water. It was crystal clear, without even the slightest trace of algae or plant matter. Filling her bottle she raised it to drink when she spied something on the far bank.

The body of a dog lay in the grass. Lowering the bottle Wilda looked further afield and saw more animal corpses in varying states of decay. Whatever had killed the villagers wasn't limited to people. Realization dawned as she reexamined the water.

It was poison. That explained it all, the abandoned village, the graves, the dead animals and the lack of organic matter. She emptied her flask as she looked upstream for any sign of the contaminant. This must be the village that Hervin had mentioned, the one that had been poisoned.

Little did she know that her every movement was being watched. A short distance across the river, a bird the size of a pigeon sat on a boulder. Beneath its faux feathers, where its eyes should have been, high definition cameras were recording and saving the footage to an internal solid-state drive.

An evolution of drone technology, the surveillance device was designed to work covertly. Intelligent, it waited for its target to cross the river and disappear into the distance before it took flight.

A casual observer would have thought nothing of the bird as it flew. However, any bird watcher would have noticed its flight pattern was unnaturally smooth. Climbing rapidly it was soon out of sight. High above the mountains, its tiny onboard transmitter established a link with its control center and uploaded the recently acquired surveillance footage.

The alert reached Crispy's wearable as he was conducting post-mission maintenance in the vehicle garage. His CPV accumulated some light wear and tear during his mission with Brad and the drilling team. One of the direct-drive hubs was showing a slight loss in power and would need replacing.

Glancing at the screen on his wrist he saw that he'd been recalled to the operations room. As he climbed out of the combat vehicle he issued an order to the maintenance system.

A hydraulic arm slid on a rail system attached to the ceiling, moving smoothly over the vehicle. A claw reached down and grasped the lifting lugs on its roof. Crispy watched as the CPV was returned to a slot in the racks that lined the walls of the garage. He'd deal with whatever Yitzhak wanted then return to ensure the maintenance was complete.

He took the long route to the command center. Strolling past the doors to the prohibited sector he hoped to catch a glimpse of anything inside. The doors were closed, and there was no one in the corridor. He paused, long enough to recheck his wearable, then continued on his way.

"You get your gear sorted?" asked Yitzhak as he entered.

"Got a little more to do on the CPV."

"Assign it to one of the techs. We're going to be busy." He gestured to the main screen, which displayed an image of a young girl by a river. "This just came in."

He immediately recognized her face, triggering an almost uncontrollable rage inside him. He could feel his face burning as he white-knuckled the chair in front of him.

"The drone didn't register a chip and I couldn't find her facial profile in the system. But, I figured you'd be able to tell me if that's your missing trainee."

Crispy nodded. He would recognize the teenager's Eurasian features anywhere. It was Eight Two, the girl he'd been sent halfway around the world to kill.

"Yeah, I thought so," said Yitzhak.

Crispy turned to face him. "Where is this? How long will it take me to get there?"

"Easy, big guy. This footage is over an hour old." The veteran Mossad operative flicked a window from his tablet up onto the center screen. "I've sent out a drone to find her."

The feed from the higher-flying surveillance asset was high resolution. Crispy could see every detail of the valley it was searching. A glance at the operations map told him it was southeast of Bismarck, only a few miles from where Brad and his team had refilled their drilling rig.

"I can get there in no time. We can kill her."

"Not when there's a capture order on her head," said Yitzhak. "And not when I've got bigger problems to deal with. The raid on Harkanass failed."

"How? We gave the marauders everything they needed to wipe them out."

"No amount of weaponry negates tactical blundering."

An alert sounded over the room's speakers, and both men turned their attention back to the primary monitor. The drone had located someone and highlighted them with a red box. Yitzhak adjusted the feed, zooming in.

He knew it was Eight Two from the way she walked. "It's definitely her."

Yitzhak shrugged. "Well, she's heading straight into trouble. That valley runs into Barzani territory."

"Barzani?"

"Not a big tribe, but the most militant in the region. If they get their hands on her, she'll wish she was dead."

"Do you have an agent there?"

Yitzhak shook his head. "No, they run a tight ship. But, like I said, they're pretty small and they're the least likely to join an insurgency. When the Kurds stood up against the Turks in '34, it was the Barzani that bore the brunt of it. The other tribes hung them out to dry. They've kept to themselves ever since."

"Do they pose a threat?"

Yitzhak shook his head. "They can rally a force of maybe fifty to a hundred, with no heavy weapons. They've got their work cut out securing their borders from marauders."

"This them?" On-screen, several indicators had appeared at the extremity of the map.

Yitzhak adjusted the feed and revealed eight figures positioned in an arc across the valley, a few hundred yards from Eight Two. "Yep, your girl's going to be hanging from the end of a rope within the hour."

"I need to send a message to Leon."

"He probably already knows."

"What, how?"

"As soon as the system matched her, it sent an encrypted HF burst to HQ."

"Addressed to who?"

Yitzhak shrugged. "How the hell would I know, it's encrypted. But I'm guessing that everyone who wants to know, now does. More to the point, we've got to un-fuck this Harkanass situation before it bites us in the ass."

Crispy's eyes had not left the screen where Eight Two was moving cautiously toward the waiting Barzani men. Yitzhak was never going to let him out until the Harkanass matter was resolved. "I'll take the mechops and deal with Harkanass. I'll wipe out what's left of the checkpoint and burn the village."

"No, that will cement the insurgency. We can't have Sakkin assets destroying villages. If we do that, our conventional forces will launch from Incirlik, and Avi Lerner will have my fucking head."

"The new mechops are low signature. I'll program them to look like marauders. We'll spearhead the attack and then let what's left of Hamdi's ragtag army deal with the village. Then, I can be ready to go after Eight Two if the Barzani haven't killed her."

Yitzhak considered the proposal. "Let's see what happens over the next twenty-four hours. Hamdi's men may have caused enough damage without committing Sakkin resources."

"We need to strike quickly."

"Look, hotshot. I've been out here for over thirty years. The last thing we want to do is rush into anything. We'll wait for my sources to report in and go from there."

Crispy knew better than to question the senior operative's decision. He turned his attention back to the screen and watched as Eight Two paused a mere couple hundred yards from her demise. His only regret that he wasn't going to be at ground level to see the look on her face.

Chapter Eight

Turkey-Kurdistan Border Region

Wilda had taken a short nap on the outskirts of the abandoned village before continuing her journey east, away from the poisoned river. She'd crossed another ridge, reaching a valley that ran in her direction of travel. Here, Wilda found a cold clear pool between two boulders. Dipping her finger she tasted the water. It was pure.

She filled her bottle then set off, following this new valley at a steady pace. By her calculations, she'd traveled half a mile down the boulder-strewn gorge before she'd sensed something was off. The hairs on the back of her neck rose as she paused and scanned her surroundings. Seeing nothing unusual she turned her attention to the sky. She had this deep-seated feeling that someone or something was watching her.

For fifteen minutes, she waited, searching for any sign of a threat. Then, tentatively, she continued her journey along the valley floor. She hadn't made it another two hundred yards before the danger appeared.

Two men, dressed in drab clothing that blended with the terrain, stepped out from behind a rocky outcrop and indicated for her to stop. She noticed their G36 assault rifles and combat carriage equipment were also painted to blend with the rocks and bushes.

"Put your pack on the ground and hold your hands up," one of them commanded in Arabic.

She shrugged the pack off her back and placed it at her feet. As she raised her hands, more men appeared from among the rocks, dressed the same.

"Put your hands behind your back," continued the man who'd spoken.

She complied, and a cord was tied securely around her wrists, binding them but not cutting off her circulation.

For three hours they marched her through the mountains before arriving at a town, not unlike Pendro. Mud-brick houses were dispersed through a valley surrounded by fruit trees and gardens. Women and children stopped and stared as she was marched through the streets. Wilda's spirits soared as she saw that many of them looked like her mother. Every second woman had high cheekbones, almond-shaped eyes and long dark hair. Was it possible that she had finally found her people?

Despite being detained and escorted, Wilda was filled with a sense of wellbeing as she walked through the village. It felt like home. She even noted that some of the dogs looked like Henry.

On the outskirts of the town the men halted at the gates to a large compound. Two escorted her inside.

The courtyard was wide, with a residence on one side where a man sat at a table. One of her guards went forward and spoke to the figure. Then, after a moment, he returned and grasped her shoulder. She was maneuvered into position opposite the man at the table.

He must be the commander, she thought. Older than the others, he was cleanly shaven with salt and pepper hair and keen grey eyes.

"Do you speak Kurdish?" he asked in his native tongue.

She nodded.

"Free her hands."

One of the guards removed the cord.

"Please, sit." He poured a cup of black tea and pushed it across the table toward her. "And drink."

She rubbed her wrists then took a sip. It was heavily laced with sugar.

"So, why did you walk into my territory, are you a spy?" he asked.

"No." Something told her that honesty was the best approach. "When I was a young girl, I was taken from my village. I'm trying to find my people."

"And you think you might be Barzani." He took a sip from his tea then held his cup with both hands.

Wilda shrugged. "It's possible."

"Or maybe you're a Sakkin spy sent by that old dog Yitzhak." He stared directly into her eyes.

"Sakkin stole me from my people. I escaped, and I'm trying—"

A loud beep interrupted her. The commander reached into his pocket and removed a device. He glanced at it then returned it to his pocket. "Go on."

"I'm trying to find my way back."

He frowned. "What is your name?"

"Wilda."

"Well, Wilda. Imagine being in my position. You have a

young woman arrive at your borders with a magical story of returning to her long-lost tribe. A young woman who no one has ever seen before. A missing child that no one ever lost. What would you think?"

"How could you be so sure?"

"My dear, I protect these people, my father protected them before me and his father before him. Nothing happens within my territory that I don't know about. Now, tell me where you came from."

"I came across the desert from Aleppo to Pendro. The people there took me in."

"If that is the case, why did you leave? The people of Pendro are good people, and now you are one of them."

"I need to find the facility where my mother was taken."

He took another sip from his tea as he studied her face. After what seemed like minutes, he spoke. "Can you describe it?"

She nodded. "If you bring me paper, I can draw it."

He nodded to one of the men standing behind him. Wilda heard him move away.

"So, what is your name?" she asked.

"I am Masrour."

The guard returned and placed a pencil and paper in front of her.

"Draw the facility," the commander said.

Wilda had only ever seen the place where her mother had been taken in her dreams. The details were hazy, but she remembered the broad outline of the concrete fortress.

Masrour watched her intently as she sketched.

When she was finished she pushed it across the table and studied his face as he inspected it. His expression revealed nothing.

He waved one of his men over. The man checked the picture, then spoke, "Bismarck."

"You know where this place is?" she asked.

Masrour rose. "Follow me."

He led her inside the residence, along a corridor and into an office. The two guards followed closely. There were screens on the wall that lit up as they entered. She waited as Masrour inputted commands into a keypad.

Wilda let out a gasp as high-resolution imagery of the facility she'd drawn appeared on the screens. "That's it. That's the exact place from my dreams."

"You've never actually seen it?"

"I think I saw it as a child. They took my mother there." She swallowed. "Have any of your people been abducted by Sakkin?"

"None. This facility that they call Bismarck has been poisoning our water for the last five years."

"I saw that. People abandoned their villages in the mountains."

Masrour nodded. "My people once farmed the entire valley all the way to the facility. Then the poison came, and they died. We have lost most of our outlying settlements and over half our people are dead."

"Sakkin have no regard for life. They spread destruction wherever they go."

"It will only get worse. They have started exploratory drilling in the mountains. Soon, if we do not fight back, we will lose everything. We must destroy the facility."

Wilda stepped closer to the screen. "You need to overwhelm the targeting system for the close defense lasers and missile packs. I'd recommend air bursting metal shards over the facility. Do you have mortars? You'll also need to defeat the ground sensors to achieve surprise. A series of shallow lifting charges will confuse them. Then you can mass your attack at a critical point, most likely the garage entrance."

Masrour frowned. "How do you know all this?"

"Because Sakkin stole me from my people and brainwashed me. They tried to turn me into one of their super soldiers... but they failed."

Sakkin HQ, South African Zone

Marnisha Copeland was staring intently at the screen of a digital microscope when her tablet announced the arrival of a priority message. The device was on the table in the middle of her spotless laboratory. She studied the tissue sample under her scope for a moment before tearing herself from the screen and checking the message.

It had come via Sakkin's high-frequency radio communications network. With satellites destroyed, the low bandwidth technology was the only way to achieve truly global communication.

Her heart skipped a beat as she read the text.

Trainee Eight Two identified vicinity Semdinli Province, Kurdistan. Captured by indigenous forces. Status unknown.

It meant that Wilda was following the path she had laid out for her, albeit quicker than anticipated. That, coupled with Sakkin's recent buildup at the old Proteus facility, had changed things somewhat. If the teenager fell into the hands of Avi Lerner or his men, it could destroy everything she had worked to create.

She drummed her manicured nails against the tablet as

she contemplated the situation. There was only one way she was going to be able to control the situation. She needed to go to Semdinli. Accessing Sakkin's transportation scheduling application she booked herself an aircraft. Then she took a travel bag she kept in her locker and left the lab.

When the doors to the elevator opened she came face to face with Avi Lerner.

"Marnisha, I was just coming to see if you wanted to join me for lunch, but I see you're on your way out."

She smiled. "I'll have to get a rain check."

"Where are you heading," he asked. "Transport hub or local?"

"The hub, please."

He pushed the button. "I had a lovely time the other night. We should do it again when you get back from…"

"I'm heading out to one of the old Proteus labs we're shutting down. I need to oversee the final transfer of data and materials to the new facility in Rwanda. I should be back in a few days, we can catch up then."

"Which lab?"

"Semdinli, I'm heading to Semdinli."

"Interesting timing," he said as the elevator came to a halt and the doors opened, revealing a lavishly appointed travel lounge.

They stepped out, and she turned to face him. "Why is that?"

"Ah, nothing specific. Just a lot of activity at what was once a backwater facility. When was the last time you visited? One, two years ago?"

She smiled, touching his shoulder. "Like I said, I'm closing the old lab. Soon, it will be all yours. I'll see you when I get back." She turned and left him at the elevator.

Avi watched her stride through the lounge and into the

main hangar. What she didn't know was that he knew the real reason she was heading to Semdinli. His insider, Crispy, had sent him a message indicating that trainee Eight Two had been located.

Marnisha's immediate departure had confirmed his suspicions. Eight Two was vital to one of her plans, and he wanted to know exactly what it was.

Riding the elevator back to his office he used his wearable to record a voice message to be sent as an HF text to Yitzhak. "The capture of Eight Two is a priority. She is to be renditioned to the interrogation facility at Incirlik."

As he entered his office on the second-highest floor, he issued a directive to his assistant. "I want Leon Wilkens and an Alpha team tasked to recover trainee Eight Two from Semdinli."

"Yes, sir. I'll task a backup team to cover Venezuela."

"Have a vertjet on standby for when they capture her. I want to be in Incirlik for the interrogation. I want to know what's in the bitch's head."

Turkey-Kurdistan Border Region

Wilda hadn't left Masrour's office since she'd arrived. He'd had food and water brought in. Then he'd grilled her for three hours on the intricacies of Sakkin security measures likely to be emplaced at the Bismarck facility.

"You've revealed more in the time I've had with you than five years of surveillance and collection," said the Barzani commander. "Allah has provided me with the mechanism to finally destroy that forsaken facility." For the first time since they had met, the old warrior smiled. "Now, tell me what you know of the internal layout."

"All I remember is a long corridor with sliding doors. I can't recall anything else. However, I do know that there will be a central operations room. If you could get me in there, I could shut everything down."

Masrour's smile faded. "You want me to take you, a stranger to my tribe, on this mission?"

Wilda nodded. "I need to get inside that facility. I need to know what happened to my mother. I need to find my people."

"Wilda, what you find inside may not be the answer you seek. You have a home now. The people of Pendro have welcomed you in. They are your family now."

"I need to know," she said quietly.

"Then, I will let you enter the facility once we have captured it. Not before. The battlefield is no place for a young woman, even one that has the intimate knowledge that you have."

Wilda fought the urge to show Masrour precisely what she could do. Instead, she bowed her head demurely. "Thank you."

"It's late. I will have my men take you to a residence. I'm sure you can understand that I need to take certain precautions."

"Of course. I appreciate your time and hospitality."

The two guards led her outside to where a pickup was waiting. They climbed into the back and drove a short distance to the outskirts of the village. As they passed houses she caught a glimpse of families going about their evening routine. It filled her with a sense of hope.

Her accommodation was a small single-story house on the edge of the village, surrounded by a high wall. The guards showed her to a modest but comfortable room with a bed, pillow and blankets. A single naked bulb hung from the ceiling. As far as safe houses went it was relatively comfortable. She sat on the edge of the bed and considered her situation.

If she stayed with the Barzani, then there was a chance they would take her to the facility. Or, now that she knew where it was, she could escape and make her own way. Yawning, she knew that decision was best made made after a good night's sleep. Her wounds were almost fully healed, but she was dead tired. Tomorrow she would work out what to do.

Bismarck Facility, Eastern Turkey

Crispy supervised the Sakkin tech as he checked the electric power unit on a battered pickup. The converted vehicle was one of three in Yitzhak's garage that he used for discreet operations. This particular truck was having problems maintaining power. So far, its shortcomings had delayed his departure to attack the checkpoint at Harkanass by over an hour. Hamdi and his remaining men would be growing impatient.

"We're going to need to swap out the drive," said the tech.

"How long will that take? I need all three vehicles for this mission."

"An hour, maybe two. It's hard to tell. These old rigs can be a pain in the ass."

"You've got forty-five minutes. Any longer, and you'll be coming with us." As he turned his back on the technician, his wearable pinged. Glancing at the screen on his wrist he saw that Yitzhak wanted him in the operations room.

As he rode the elevator he wondered if there had been a development in the situation. The drone monitoring the checkpoint had revealed it was still being manned by reinforcements from another village. Twenty dirt farmers armed with AKs would not be a match for his mechop squad.

"Your mission has changed," Yitzhak said as Crispy entered the operations room. "Avi Lerner wants trainee Eight Two captured."

Crispy couldn't help but smile. Finally, he was going to get his chance. "Do we still have a fix on her?"

"Yes. That's why we're going to move tonight. Lerner is sending a team, but I can't guarantee we'll know where she is by the time they arrive."

"We can handle it."

Yitzhak pointed to the main screen, currently showing a map of the region. "The drone tracked her to a location on the outskirts of Barzani. You'll have to pass through at least one checkpoint to get to it. A single vehicle will attract less attention. How many mechops will you need?"

"How many guards at the checkpoint and the target?"

"Two at the checkpoint, at least three at the target building. The Barzani will have a QRF, maybe ten more men."

"I can do it with two mechops."

Yitzhak nodded. "I'll position a CPV with additional clankers short of the checkpoint for support. If you hit any trouble, they can back you up."

"When do I leave?"

"As soon as you're ready. I want her in custody and awaiting the arrival of the rendition team by dawn. I'll contact Hamdi and tell him there will be a delay of the attack on Harkanass."

"He won't like that."

"I'll sweeten the deal. You focus on capturing the girl."

"I can launch now."

"Good." Yitzhak grasped the younger man's shoulder. "Son, you get this done, and I'll get permission to get that eye fixed."

"Just the eye. I don't want my face changed."

The veteran smirked. "Yeah, you own that Crispy shit. Now, get the hell on the road."

Turkey-Kurdistan Border Region

Crispy watched the Barzani checkpoint on a screen inside his CPV. Parked in the darkness a mile distant, the vehicle's integrated drone feed was showing him real-time imagery of the target.

He could see that there were two men on duty, manning a machine gun in a sandbagged outpost. The high-resolution feed revealed one of them was wearing night-vision goggles. From what he'd seen, the Barzani militia was a coordinated, well-trained and well-equipped force.

"Execute," he ordered over his radio.

One of his clankers, hidden on a hill less than five hundred feet from the checkpoint, fired two rounds in rapid succession. In low power mode, the railer was a stealthy weapon. The two bolts impacted within milliseconds of each other, punching through the sentrys' skulls with surgical precision.

Crispy stepped out of the CPV and climbed in behind the wheel of the battered pickup. He was dressed in the traditional robes of the region. Underneath, however, he was clad in nano-armor capable of protecting him from everything but the heaviest of gunfire. On the seat beside him was the latest generation of compact railer. In the bed of the pickup was one of Avi Lerner's covert mechops, its adaptive exterior set to resemble an elderly traveler.

With headlights off and in electric mode, he accelerated toward the checkpoint. As he drove along the road Crispy considered the nickname that operatives used to describe their robotic foot soldiers. Clankers had seemed appropriate when they'd been hulking steel combatants bristling with armament. These covert mechops needed a different name, something that described their stealthy nature and ability to disguise themselves. He liked the term shapeshifter, but it was a little long. Shifter, he thought, shifter is the perfect name.

He arrived at the checkpoint as his first shifter appeared from inside the adjacent bunkhouse.

"All entities eliminated," it reported via radio comms.

He slowed, allowing it to leap into the bed of the truck. Then he accelerated along the road that led to the target area. The vehicle's dash was digital and highlighted the route. It also showed him the live stream from the drone that was hovering over the building. So far, there had been minimal movement. Considering it was three in the morning, he didn't expect that to change anytime soon. His plan was to get in fast, grab the bitch and get out. If things went hot, he could call in fire from the CPV and deploy the additional shifters. He was confident he could handle anything the Barzani could throw at him.

Chapter Nine

Turkey-Kurdistan Border Region

A high-pitched bark woke Wilda from a deep, dreamless sleep, and her thoughts immediately turned to Henry, the dog she had rescued. She wondered if he was currently curled up on the end of Xeyal's or Behdin's bed. Most likely, Xeyal. She definitely had a soft spot for the little hound.

The barking outside increased in intensity before it stopped abruptly. Wilda pulled back the blankets and swung her legs off the bed. Slipping her boots on she pulled the laces tight. Hairs on the back of her neck rose as she left the bed and tried the door to her room. It was locked.

Masrour's men had left her backpack. She checked inside it and found that everything was still there, aside from the Glock and her spare magazine. They'd even filled her water bottle and added a few pieces of fruit. After a moment of rummaging she found a clasp knife. They'd practiced break and enter training at the *Institute*, everything from tumblers to electronic access pads. With one of the knife's blades she made short work of the lock and tentatively pushed the door open.

There was no one in the hall outside. Stealing along the corridor she peeked into one of the rooms. It was a kitchen. Moving toward the front door she caught a whiff of cigarette smoke. Pausing, she considered returning to her room. The dog outside was probably barking at a jackal. Then she heard a sound that was all too familiar, the hiss of a railer on low power.

She turned and ran to the rear of the building, searching for an exit. Behind, she heard the front door swing open. Glancing over her shoulder she saw a figure standing in the doorway, Seven Nine Nine.

"Where the fuck do you think you're going?"

Wilda found the back door and burst through it into the darkness. Skidding around the corner she nearly collided with an elderly man in robes. He moved with uncanny swiftness, grabbing her arm in a vice-like grip.

"Let me go!" she yelled, twisting her arm as she shoved him. To her surprise, her palm didn't meet flesh and cloth. The man's body was encased in a rigid shell. When her arm didn't wrench free she drove her elbow into the side of his bearded face. It bounced on a hard surface, jarring her shoulder. "What the hell."

Panic overwhelmed her as she realized it wasn't a man, but a clanker of some kind. It lunged for her other arm. She snatched it clear as she spun, wrapping her legs around the machine's neck and toppling it off balance. Breaking her arm free she leaped catlike to one side.

The machine recovered quicker than any clanker she'd ever seen. It flipped back onto its feet as she scrambled away.

Another figure appeared. Wilda ran up the wall, sprung

away and grasped the edge of the building. Flipping onto the roof she rolled onto her front then dashed across the smooth concrete.

She heard one of the robots behind her as she leaped from the roof. Clearing the external wall she landed heavily in the field that bordered the makeshift prison.

A whirring above revealed that a drone had detected her. Staggering to her feet she spotted a row of trees less than a hundred yards distant and sprinted for them.

She sensed the blast of electrical energy a split second before it hit her. Pain shot through her body as it rendered her muscles useless, and she fell to the ground convulsing.

"Finally, we've caught the rat." She recognized Seven Nine Nine's voice. "Now you're going to pay."

He appeared above her, grinning maniacally as his gloved hand closed around her throat.

"Oh, you're going to pay."

The sharp sting of an auto-injector was the last thing she felt before her world went black.

Crispy felt a sense of elation as he cuffed Eight Two with carbon fiber binders. Ever since he'd been removed from the *Institute* and exiled to South America, he had dreamed of this moment. With any luck Sakkin would promote him from Trainee to Operative.

A shifter carried Eight Two to the pickup and dumped her into the bed, before climbing in with its partner.

Behind the wheel of the electric-powered truck Crispy checked the drone feed of the checkpoint. The Barzani militia had found their dead men and reinforced with a squad of infantry. If he tried to run the defensive position there was a chance that a stray bullet could hit Eight Two. If that happened, then he could say goodbye to his status being upgraded, and his ruined eye replaced.

As he accelerated silently along the return route he issued a command to his CPV, still parked on the other side of the checkpoint. Driving with his lights off he relied on what remained of his enhanced vision to navigate the roads. A half-mile from the checkpoint he skidded to a halt.

The drone feed showed that the men at the checkpoint were orientated in both directions. There was no way through it without getting shot up. He smirked as he jabbed an icon on his wearable with his finger.

Accelerating smoothly he counted down the seconds. He was a few hundred yards from the checkpoint when the munitions hit. Two missiles fired from the CPV detonated above the Barzani squad, shredding them with tungsten pellets.

He stomped the accelerator to the floor and the pickup sped through the carnage, bouncing over the bodies strewn across the road. Driving at high speed he rapidly covered the mile to where the CPV and his additional shifters were waiting. They pulled in behind him as he passed.

"We have the package, and we're en-route to Bismarck," he transmitted.

"Good work. Now we can get back to disrupting the Harkanass treaty."

He couldn't help but smile as he headed back to the facility. Things were finally looking up for him. Not so much for Eight Two. He'd seen what happened to people during a Sakkin interrogation. She'd be fortunate to come out of this alive, but if she did, he would ask Avi Lerner for the pleasure of terminating her.

The tunnel ran from an empty home not far from the residence where Mansour had questioned Wilda. He followed a string of lights for five hundred yards before emerging into a expansive cave, an abandoned zinc mine.

One of his men met him in another tunnel that had been enlarged to house vehicles and equipment. "Sir, initial reports indicate that a hostile element penetrated our territory and snatched the girl," reported his lieutenant.

"How many casualties?"

"Thirteen. No wounded."

The veins in Masrour's jaw bulged as he clenched his teeth. "They will pay." He strode down the tunnel, passing stacks of ammunition and weapon boxes. "The mortar rounds. Have they been modified?"

"They'll be done by morning. The commanders are waiting for you."

Masrour turned into a smaller tunnel that led into a concrete bunker. There was a table in the middle of the room with five men seated at it. He and his lieutenant joined them. "I take it you're all across what happened last night?" He glanced at his watch. "Correction, this morning."

The men nodded solemnly.

"What are we going to do about it?" asked one of them.

"The girl they took gave me information," said Masrour.

"You mean the spy they recovered," said the same man.

The commander shrugged. "I considered that, but I think it's more likely that they snatched her because of what she knows. They killed thirteen of our men to keep her secrets. We're going to use her information to make them pay."

Bismarck Facility, Eastern Turkey

Wilda exhaled slowly as she woke from a dreamless sleep. For a moment, she thought she was still in the Barzani safe house. Then, as the haze of the sedative lifted, she recalled the moments before her capture and realized she was in deep trouble.

The small cell spun as she sat up. Bile flooded her mouth, and she searched frantically for something to vomit into. There was a toilet mounted on the wall, and she lurched over, managing to get most of the puke into it.

Gasping for air she leaned against the cell's smooth walls and gathered herself. The urge to vomit abated after a few seconds of deep breathing, giving her the chance to take in her surroundings.

From the size of the room, the thickness of the solid glass front, and the amenities, she knew she was in a standard Sakkin detention cell. That meant she was probably a long way from Barzani territory.

"Ready for breakfast?"

The voice sent a shiver through her body. Trainee Seven Nine Nine appeared behind the cell's glass wall.

She immediately noticed that his molten features had changed. His face was still damaged, but now the scarring looked superficial. His missing eye had been replaced with a white eyeball. The overall effect was unnerving, a face that was no longer human.

"You like the new look?" he said, noticing her lingering

stare. "Yeah, you did a real number on me. But now I've got a serious enhancement." He tapped his new eye. "This bad boy's got everything a helmet would: heads-up display, weapon targeting, thermal vision. You've turned me into the ultimate operative."

She shook her head. "Can't you see what they're doing to you?"

He smashed his fist on the glass between them. "No, you fucking did this to me. You ruined my life and Tree's. You're poison, Eight Two, but now it's over."

"Is he alive?" she asked.

Crispy ignored the question. "They're sending a rendition team. You're going to tell them everything they want to know, and then they're going to toss you in the trash."

"Seven, they're using all of us."

He sneered. "Crispy, my name's Crispy."

As he turned to leave, she asked one last question. "Where am I?"

He paused. "They call it Bismarck, but to you, it's going to be hell." He shot her a wink as he left. "Have fun. I'll be watching."

Wilda slumped to the floor of the cell in disbelief. She was inside the facility where they'd taken her mother. This was the place from her dreams. Placing her palms against the wall, she exhaled. Finally, she'd found something from her childhood, something real.

Gathering herself, she began studying every part of the cell. If she was going to find out what happened to her mother, she needed a way out.

She focused her attention on the glass door, checking it's locking mechanism and hinges for potential weakness. Tracing her fingers over the thick transparent material she felt a slight vibration. The panel shimmered as a tremor rippled through the cell. It only lasted a split second, but it was enough to give Wilda a sense of hope.

"What was that?" asked Crispy as the facility's threat sensor interface flashed up on the main screen of the operations room. Ground sensors for miles around the facility were reporting movement.

"Earth tremor, we get them from time to time. The sensors will reset when it subsides." Yitzhak glanced at Crispy. "That new eye looks good on you."

He nodded. "Greatly appreciated."

"Deserved, you did a good job. Now, we've got two aircraft due in the next three hours."

"Two?"

"The rendition team and Marnisha Copeland, Sakkin's top scientist. This was her facility."

"She comes here often?"

"Twice in the ten years I've been here."

Crispy frowned. "Why now?"

"They've been shutting this place down. Moving all the bio shit to another lab somewhere. Allegedly, she's coming to move the last of her samples."

"They told me that she modified trainee Eight Two, and that's why she escaped."

"What, like messed with her brain?"

He nodded.

"That's fucked up." Yitzhak paused. "You think she's coming to pick up her pet project?" He glanced at his tablet. "She's going to arrive before the rendition team. Technically, once she's here, I have to do everything she asks."

"Then, we need to slow her down," said Crispy.

The main screen flashed again, more tremors.

Yitzhak winked. "Unfortunately, that last shake damaged our autonomous landing array. Our technicians are working to bring it back online."

Crispy chuckled.

A high-pitched alarm interrupted their conspiring, followed by a calm female voice. "Incoming rounds. Activating HEAPS."

HEAPS, or the High Energy Anti Projectile System, was an automated laser powered by the fusion reactor deep within the fortress. Crispy had seen the weapons turrets and radar domes on the roof when he'd arrived.

Yitzhak used his tablet to display the threat screen on the primary monitor. The HEAPS had painted red target indicators on several mortar rounds arcing toward them. "Where the fuck did they come from?"

Crispy watched with rapt attention as the bombs descended, anticipating the lasers that would detonate the warheads high above them. Then suddenly, they exploded prematurely.

"What the hell?" snapped Yitzhak.

The threat screen filled with thousands of red markers. Bolts of energy filled the sky as the HEAPS lasers went wild.

"They've overloaded the system," snarled Yitzhak.

The screen went blank, and a moment later, the building shook as a high explosive round struck it.

"Launch our drones," ordered the veteran as the building shook again. "Crispy, get to the armory and bring all the mechops online. I'm going to contact Hamdi and find out who the hell is attacking us."

"We should pay him to hit them from a flank," said Crispy.

"You're finally starting to think like an operative. Now,

get your team ready. Something tells me there's plenty of killing to be done."

"It worked. It worked," yelled Masrour as he watched high explosives rain down on the Sakkin facility through powerful binoculars.

His mortar teams had slipped past the ground sensors under cover of explosive ground charges simulating earth tremors. It was all part of the plan that Wilda had given him before Sakkin had snatched her. She'd identified a series of weaknesses in the fortress's defense that would allow his forces to destroy Bismarck, stop the flow of poison and reclaim his territories.

Thumbing the transmit button on his radio he issued a command, "Send in the breaching vehicle."

As he issued the order, he spotted a series of disc-shaped drones shooting out of the concrete fortress. At least one of them exploded, caught by a mortar blast. The others zoomed skyward, beginning a search pattern.

"Stinger teams target the drones. Mortar teams take cover." His enemy was continuing to respond precisely how Wilda had predicted.

His breaching vehicle was an up-armored 4x4, modified for remote control. Its critical task was to destroy the garage doors of the concrete monolith so his assault force could penetrate its depths. They would then lure out Sakkin's deadly robots so his weapons teams could attack them with anti-armor rockets and heavy machine guns.

As the breaching vehicle sped toward the fortress leaving a trail of dust, a rocket streaked skyward from a ridge to his right. The stinger missile detonated in a ball of shrapnel, tearing another drone from the sky.

"Masrour," said his lieutenant. "Vehicles are approaching from the north east. Sakkin may have called for reinforcements."

"How? Their closest base is eight hundred miles away."

"Marauders, we don't have the manpower to fight them and assault the fortress at the same time."

At that moment, a massive ball of smoke and dust rolled up from the front of the Sakkin facility. A split second later, the sound of the explosion hit them.

"We've breached," announced Masrour. "Split the assault teams. Have half of them ambush the marauders. Once they've finished them, they can join the assault."

"The girl didn't predict this," said his lieutenant. "The whole thing could have been a trap to draw us out and annihilate us."

Masrour pondered the comment. "I doubt that. We've already cost them dearly."

"A few drones and some laser modules is a cheap price to wipe out a force like ours."

"You think we should withdraw?" asked Masrour.

"Yes, before we regret it."

The Barzani commander clenched his teeth. "Destroy the marauders and press home the attack. We will never get this chance again."

Located directly above the garage complex, Bismarck's detention facility had borne a significant amount of the force from the breaching explosion. The blast had shoved the floor upwards, throwing Wilda against the ceiling.

Slamming back onto the floor she lay dazed, coughing dust-laden air as alarms wailed. Pulling her t-shirt up over her mouth she staggered to her feet and checked the door to the cell.

The explosion had dislodged the panel of thick perspex from its frame, leaving a one-inch gap that she could slip her fingers under. Bracing against the floor she pulled with all her strength.

The frame creaked, shifted slightly, then wedged firm.

"Come on." She reset her feet, exhaled, and tried again. The door shuddered as she pulled with all her strength. Blackness crept into the edges of her vision, and her muscles screamed in protest. Finally, the door twisted, opening a small gap. Dropping to her knees she slid her arms into the space and wriggled her shoulders through. She pushed back with her arms and squeezed through, dropping into a narrow corridor.

There were six cells in total, all of them empty. The corridor ended at a security door that had also been damaged by the explosion. It took her a moment to pry the door open and slip out into the pandemonium.

Alarms wailed, lights flickered and the stench of burning plastic was thick in the air. She stole along a long passage toward what she hoped was the center of the complex. She needed to find a computer terminal or a building diagram to help navigate her way around.

The sound of boots slapping on the floor halted her and she looked around for a way out. The doors on either side were locked. Panicked, she turned and sprinted in the opposite direction. She almost ran headfirst into three white-garbed men. One of them grabbed her shoulders.

"Hey, are you alright? We're all heading to the mess hall. It's the other way."

Wilda realized that covered from head to toe in dust, she was completely unrecognizable.

"I'm OK. What's happening?" she stammered as a pair of security personnel rushed past.

"We're under attack," said the man. "The mess hall is the rally point for all noncoms. It's the strongest part of the building."

"OK, I need to check on one of my colleagues. Can you point me in the direction of the med bay?"

The man frowned. "Are you with the Sumsunto team? You should have been told during induction."

She nodded. "I'm just a little disorientated."

"OK, I'll take you." He turned to the others. "I'll catch up with you guys at the mess."

He led her along the corridor and through a security door into another section of the facility. "Seriously, we were due out in two days. I've been here for four years, and there's never been an incident. You guys start drilling, and it all turns to shit."

"The luck of the draw," she replied. "What do you do?"

"I work in the lab. We're the last of the techs. Everyone else has already shipped out."

They arrived at a door marked with a red cross. "OK, this is it. While you're here, get yourself checked out and then head to the mess. I'll see you there." He held out his hand. "Name's Trav."

She grasped it and shook it. "I'm Wilda, thanks."

She entered the aid post alone and was surprised to find it empty. A medical robot registered her presence and gestured for her to sit in a comfortable medical recliner. "Trainee Eight Two, please sit so I can carry out a full-body scan."

Wilda was shocked to hear her trainee designator, but

then remembered she still had an ID chip embedded in her head. "No, thank you," she said as she activated a touch screen terminal.

"That terminal is for medical personnel only," the medop stated.

Wilda knew the Sakkin system more intimately than most. Henry, a technician with the company, had taught her the basics, and then she had burrowed deep into the code. It took her a matter of seconds to hack the administrative systems. From there, she accessed a detailed floor plan. Identifying her location she looked for anything that seemed familiar. The floor she was on contained living quarters, the mess hall, medical facilities and the prison.

She checked the floor above and saw there was nothing listed. The entire level was blank. Reviewing the security protocols she noted that the zone had strict access controls. Whatever was inside must be of great importance, and something told her it was where they had taken her mother.

"Please cease your actions, or I will be forced to inform security," announced the medical robot.

Wilda sighed, found the clanker in the system, and activated sleep mode. Then she programmed her own identification code into the security system, removing the tracking function but enabling her to move through the standard access areas. Getting into the restricted zone was something she would have to tackle when she got there.

Chapter Ten

Bismarck Facility, Eastern Turkey

An RPG round slammed into the wall above Crispy sending hot shards of metal bouncing off the armor of his berserker suit. The heavy-duty exoskeleton was an older model, but more than capable of protecting him from everything but a direct hit from an enhanced warhead. He and his squad of shifters and older mechops had formed a defensive position in the garage, covering the massive hole that the attackers had blasted through the reinforced door.

So far, not a single attacker had managed to penetrate Bismarck. A half-dozen bodies littered the opening and the ground beyond, shredded by railers and grenade launchers.

"They've shot down our remaining drones," reported Yitzhak over his communications link. "We're now blind to what's happening out there. I need you and the mechops to push out and establish a perimeter around the facility. From there, we can hunt down the mortars."

"And the marauders?"

"The last I saw, they were under attack and being decimated. We're facing a capable foe. They knew exactly where to hit us."

"Barzani?"

There was a pause. "It seems we have severely underestimated their capabilities."

"That bitch, Eight Two, probably told them everything they needed."

"The rendition team arrives in two hours. We need to clean this mess up before they get here. Deploy the mechops and the CPVs, slaughter the Barzani dogs, Crispy."

"It will be done." He fired a volley of smoke grenades through the opening of the garage. The thermal imaging in his helmet gave him clear vision. He ordered his clankers forward. Their railers hissed, and more smoke grenades popped as they extended the screen of thick black smoke.

Crispy doubted that many, if any, of the attackers had thermal imaging equipment. The smoke would obscure him and his mechops, while they targeted the enemy using multi-spectral sensors.

He ordered the heavy clankers to establish a perimeter, a short distance from the facility. They commenced blasting anything that registered on their sensors. He gave them a moment before following in his berserker suit.

His metal boots crushed a dead Barzani soldier as he exited the breach and strode through the smoke onto the alternate landing zone that fronted the garage. It was littered with the remains of the massive car bomb that had breached the doors.

A mechop to his right fired a volley of railer penetrators at the valley wall a half-mile away. A split second later an explosion erupted as an enemy heavy weapon detonated.

"Shifters, adopt local camouflage profile, hunt and

destroy all hostile elements," he ordered as he positioned himself behind a sizable boulder.

He watched as the six humanoid robots stole into the rocks, their nanoskin adopting a pattern that blended perfectly with the landscape. The heads-up display built into his helmet painted them with blue icons so he could track them as they made their way up the mountainside. It wouldn't take them long to eradicate the attackers.

"Move two CPVs out to provide fire support," he ordered.

The automated vehicles exited the garage through the gap in the doors and stopped either side of the pad, their missile launchers raised.

As his shifters climbed the mountain, he followed in his exoskeleton, clambering over rocks a few hundred yards behind.

A heavy machine gun thumped, and one of the advanced mechops announced it had been damaged. The map in his helmet showed him where the gun had fired from, and he tagged it for a missile launch.

Almost immediately one of the CPVs released a single rocket that streaked over his head and slammed into a vehicle attempting to escape along a dirt track. Weapons and crates of ammunition lay abandoned across the spur line.

"The Barzani are withdrawing," he reported to Yitzhak as he ordered the CPVs to pick him and the shifters up. "Request permission to pursue and destroy."

"Negative," responded Yitzhak. "You need to get back here. That little bitch of yours has escaped from detention. She's loose in the facility. I'm locking the place down."

For a split second, Crispy was furious, but then it

dawned on him. Now, he had the opportunity to hunt her down and terminate her. "I'm on my way."

Turkey-Kurdistan Border Region

Masrour helped unload a man strapped to a stretcher then watched for a moment as a medic applied a dressing to a savage shrapnel wound in the casualty's thigh. He was one of the lucky ones. A lot of his men had been killed during the failed attack on Bismarck. Leaving the aid post he walked deeper into the mine that housed his forces, or at least what remained of them.

"Our losses?" he asked his lieutenant as he entered the command center.

"Eleven dead, so far. Not all men are accounted for. Also, we lost most of our heavy weapons."

"And the facility?"

"Its primary defenses were neutralized but we failed to penetrate the breach."

The Barzani commander exhaled as he slumped into his chair. "We failed."

His lieutenant nodded. "But so did they. We have retained most of our men. Weapons can be replaced."

"How do you fight wraiths? They were on the battlefield for minutes, and they tore through us like we were nothing. I've never seen technology like that."

"The girl led us into an ambush."

Masrour was silent.

"We can get better weapons. We can be better prepared," his lieutenant continued as the door to the bunker swung open, and the team leaders entered.

"Where is Razim?" asked Masrour.

One of the men shook his head. "He did not make it."

They gathered around the table, and Masrour addressed them. "Today was not the great victory we wanted, but it was not a total loss. We took on an enemy far stronger than us. We bloodied his nose and, despite losing good men, we were not defeated. You all fought hard, and you fought well. This will not be our last battle against the Sakkin dogs."

"What do we do now?" asked one of his men.

"Now, we rebuild. People have made contact with us who can supply more sophisticated weapons."

The man who spoke snorted. "Good samaritans with empty promises? No, we need to form a pact with the Shia warlords. They have tanks and artillery."

"You saw the drones and the missiles. They would destroy tanks before they got close enough to fight," said Masrour. "We need lighter, more lethal technology, and we need more of it. Razim and the others will not have died in vain. We will make them pay, and we will take back our lands."

Bismarck Facility, Eastern Turkey

Wilda remembered the corridor from her dreams. It was etched in her memory like a eulogy on a tombstone. Her mother had been screaming as they wheeled her through the opaque glass doors engraved with the words, *Restricted Area*.

She'd accessed the second floor through the ventilation system, a process that had almost reduced her to tears. It was how she'd first met Henry at the *Institute*. She'd hacked the training facility's life-support systems to escape her room and explore. It had been the start of her first real friendship. It seemed only fitting that Henry would play another part in revealing her origins.

Checking the tablet she'd taken from the med bay she saw the only way to open the door was to directly access its hard wire. She examined the wall alongside, tapping the surface as she worked away from the door. When it sounded hollow she punched her fist through the thin exterior sheet. Ripping a sheet of plastic material from the wall she exposed the metal framing beneath. Reaching into the cavity she found the wiring, shorted it and gained access.

She'd expected a hospital. However, the area behind the door looked more like a factory floor than a medical facility. In a large room she found rows of strange-looking pods with operating terminals on the walls. A mechanical arm hung from a track on the roof.

"What is this place?" she whispered, inspecting one of the pods. The container was the size of a large trash can. It sat on an angle, its smooth white sides blending into a clear window. Peering inside she saw it was empty. She searched for a label on the machine, and found it down low where it was plugged into cords and tubes that ran into the floor. A small plate had a serial number and a name on it. She read it and her blood ran cold.

Sakkin Industries - Artificial Womb X18745

This wasn't a hospital; it was a factory where they produced children. The revelation hit her like a freight train, smashing through every layer of self-identity that she'd managed to construct since her escape from the *Institute*.

She wasn't a child, stolen from a family and a village. This here had been her beginning, grown in a plastic bubble to deal out death and destruction on behalf of corporate masters. She wasn't the orphan of long-dead parents. She was an organic machine constructed in a sterile factory by lab-coated technicians like Trav.

A sense of gut-wrenching despair grew inside her as she walked along the rows of artificial wombs. As she reached the end of a row she realized that everyone at the *Institute* could have come from this place. She wasn't even unique, just another cog in Sakkin's giant grinding machine.

There was an adjoining room on the far side of the factory floor. Standing in front of a pane of hardened glass she looked into what had to be the laboratory. Strange machines, computers and shelves of medical containers lined the space. She needed to get inside. Her previous trick wasn't going to work against solid reinforced walls. There had to be another way.

She remembered the crane attached to the roof. The hydraulic arm would have been used to move the heavy artificial wombs. A quick scan of the factory located a control panel on a far wall. The arm would take its commands from within the laboratory but the control panel was a redundancy in case there was an accident.

Thanks to Henry's training she made short work of the arm's security profiles and sent it sliding along the rail. Then, she selected a womb. The claw's hydraulic fingers fitted into a lifting bracket at the rear of the plastic bubble and hefted it effortlessly from the floor, tearing it free of cables and wires.

Moving it to the opposite end to the laboratory she lined it up with the window and sent it trundling toward it. Frustrated by its slow progress, she jammed the controls and met it halfway across the room. Shouldering the dome she powered it forward and managed to double its speed.

When the heavy object hit the window, Wilda expected it to shatter. Instead, the glass held, but the window frame popped inward.

She climbed through the gap and began exploring the laboratory. Most of the equipment was alien to her, but she did manage to find the tablet interface for the factory of wombs. It didn't take her long to access the system and reveal the process for generating a child. It looked as if blank embryos were developed off-site and stored in cryogenic tubes before they were uploaded with genetic profiles and installed in the womb. According to the protocols, the profiles included memory data to shape personality development.

Wilda felt utterly numb as she realized everything that had driven her toward this facility was a lie. Her mother had never been brought here, because she never had a mother or a father. Someone in Sakkin had designed every last piece of her, from her physique to her motivations and deepest desires.

Everything she'd ever dreamed was a lie, concocted by Sakkin to shape her toward their objectives. But, she'd broken that paradigm, and like Masrour had said, now she had a family and a people of her own. Now she was on her own path.

She searched through the system for any indication of where the genetic profiles were stored. If she could find hers, then she could know everything that Sakkin had planned for her.

According to the system, the profiles were stored in a dedicated vault. Abandoning the terminal she searched the lab and found it in the far corner. The size of a vending machine, it worked in a similar manner. A keypad demanded a four-digit number. She punched in her Sakkin trainee number, Zero Zero Eight Two. To her surprise the machine hummed, a small drawer popped open, revealing a flat silver disk the size of a quarter.

Wilda recognized the item as a proxy drive. When placed on a receiver, it allowed someone to access the data contained within. She slipped it into her pocket. Now that she had answers, she needed to find a way out.

Crispy parked his hulking berserker suit in the smoking garage and commanded it to open. The back of the armored suit peeled apart like the petals of a flower, and he stepped out, wearing lightweight armor and his comms earpiece.

"Where the hell is she?" he yelled as he strode across to a CPV and snatched a submachine railer from inside.

"She's somewhere on level three. Somehow she penetrated the restricted area and disabled the biometric tracking," replied Yitzhak through his earpiece.

"I'll kill her."

"I need you to hold firm. We've got company landing on the secondary pad."

"The rendition team?"

"No, that bitch Copeland. She overrode the lockout. The rendition team is still another thirty minutes out."

A roar from outside the garage doors confirmed that an aircraft was landing. Downwash blew dust and debris inside as a vertjet appeared and descended to the alternate landing pad. Touching down, the thrusters shut off.

The ramp dropped, and a woman dressed in heels and a

suit strode through the smoke into the garage. She made her way directly to Crispy.

"What the hell happened here?" Copeland asked.

"We were attacked by a rebel force. A traitor has penetrated the facility. I'm about to neutralize her."

Her eyes narrowed. "You're the one she escaped from in Homs. The one who was burnt. You're supposed to be in Venezuela with that idiot Wilkens."

Crispy struggled to hide the rage from his voice. "She won't get away from me this time."

"We'll see. Now, escort me to the lab."

He directed her to the elevator, ordering two of his shifters to join them. The mechops shimmered as they morphed from camouflaged killers into security personnel.

"Impressive toys," Copeland said as they entered the elevator. "Is Yitzhak holed up in the operations room?"

"Yes, he's monitoring the external threats," replied Crispy as they stopped on the third floor and the doors opened. He gestured for the two shifters to move ahead and clear the corridor. Then, he followed with his weapon raised.

"Is this necessary?" asked Copeland.

He lowered the railer. "I can stand them down, if that's what you want."

"It's fine, just get a move on."

They moved along the corridor to the doors that he'd never been able to enter. They were wide open.

"Stay here," ordered Copeland.

"What if Eight Two is in there?"

"Stay! Keep your clankers out of my lab." Copeland left the security team in the hall and entered the obsolete facility. Her eye was immediately drawn to the laboratory at the far end of the factory floor. The technicians who'd installed the facility had assured her it was impenetrable. Clearly, that wasn't the case. Her ID chip gave her access through the door. Someone, most likely Eight Two, had used a more unorthodox method of entry.

Taking a tablet from her purse, she used it to access the lab's security log. Hidden cameras confirmed that Eight Two had been here. She watched as the girl used another tablet to reveal the secrets of the lab, then access her digital imprint from the vault.

"Clever girl," she said as she walked to the vault and inputted a command in the keypad. The device hummed for a second then deposited a proxy drive into her hand. She slipped it into her purse and inputted a second command.

The vault emitted a high-pitched whine that escalated in intensity before culminating with a loud thump. With that action, she'd ended the usefulness of the laboratory. The disk in her bag held the digital imprint of every ganic ever grown here, thousands of profiles designed to produce the ultimate operative. The archaic technology had helped her perform one last task, but now she was done with it.

"I'm going to the operations room," she said as she emerged from the lab.

"Do you need me to escort you?" asked Crispy.

"I'm sure you've got something better to do," she snapped as she made for the elevator. Part of her was hoping that she'd run into Eight Two on her way. The girl was, without a doubt, the most impressive product that this facility had ever created.

Yitzhak met her at the door to the operations room. He would have been tracking her via her Sakkin ID and the CCTV network.

"Did you get what you came for?" he asked as she strode in and stood in front of the main screen.

"Yes. It would seem that my decision to close the lab was fortuitous. The neighborhood seems to have taken a turn for the worse."

"You wouldn't know anything about that, would you?"

"What are you implying?"

"Trainee Eight Two appears in my AO and suddenly a revolution breaks out."

"I was led to believe you had her detained."

"And we will again. Now, if there's nothing else. I have work to do."

Copeland smiled. "I think I'll stay. That way, if you do recover the asset, she can be returned to my custody for further development."

It was Yitzhak's turn to smile. "Well, you'll have to take that up with Director Lerner. I mean, this facility falls under his directorate now and…" He nodded toward the air movements tracking map on a wall screen. "His rendition team will be on the ground in less than thirty minutes."

Wilda watched the woman in the lab through the slats of a ventilation grate. She'd seen her before at the *Institute*. The Sakkin official was beautiful and held herself in a way that radiated authority. Her presence suggested she might be the one behind the program, the person creating the personality profiles for an army of fabricated ganics.

She contemplated dropping from the vent and confronting her, but realized that would be a futile act. The answers as to why Sakkin grew its own operatives were evident. It gave them total control over a replaceable asset that they could treat like property.

It explained the ruthless lethality of her fellow trainees at the *Institute*. Sakkin had programmed them from inception to have zero empathy and remorse. They were unable to relate to anything other than the undying commitment to the mission. She wondered what had gone wrong with her? How was it that she was capable of feeling when all the other trainees were unemotional robots?

She waited till the woman had finished in the lab and departed before she continued squirming through the ventilation tubing. Her plan was to make her way back to a vertical shaft and climb down to the garage level. From there, she would find a way to slip out of the facility.

As she shimmied along a duct her thoughts turned to Behdin, Xeyal and the village of Pendro. Behdin's parents had accepted her into their family, and she had a little dog that would be missing her. Yet she'd left the village to protect them from Sakkin, and now, in the place where she was supposed to find answers, she felt utterly alone.

Pressing her body into the side of a vertical vent she braced her feet against the wall opposite and slowly descended toward the garage. Reaching the lower levels she paused at a junction. She could feel that air was being pulled past her into the power generation plant. The building's schematics told her that the facility's power, water and waste plant were in that direction. That's where the pollution from the reactor would be entering the river.

If she could find an explosive charge she could sabotage the plant and shut down the facility. The garage would have combat vehicles, probably CPVs, and she knew where the weapons and grenades were stored in them.

From inside the ducting she could hear activity on the

garage floor. Peering through a vent she saw there were clankers positioned, covering the destroyed doors. Maintenance robots were clearing away debris. There was no sign of Crispy or any other ganics, as far as she could see.

The ducting ran across the roof of the cavernous space. Wilda identified that the far vent was only a few feet above the vehicle storage shelving, a suitable exit. As she slid through the dusty piping, she suppressed a sneeze. Then, when she was halfway, there was a loud groan, and the metal duct shuddered. She stopped with her heart in her mouth. If the pipe dropped, then the fall was going to injure, if not kill her.

After a few seconds the noise subsided, so she continued edging slowly forward until she reached the vent above the vehicles. The plastic slotted grill provided little resistance and she managed to twist it free from its mounts. She let it drop a few feet onto the roof of an electric utility vehicle. Then she lowered herself after it, hiding behind the cabin of the small truck.

From her vantage point, she could see the destruction that Masrour's attack had managed to inflict on the Sakkin facility. The floor was littered with debris, including the parts of at least two older style mechops. The massive blast doors had been breached cleanly. She wondered why Masrour and his men hadn't pressed home the attack. If they'd managed to breach, it meant that the facility's external defenses had been disabled.

A quick scan of the room identified what she was looking for. There were two CPVs on the level below her. The framework that housed the vehicles was open with channels that supported their wheels. It was easy to climb down through the struts onto the roof of the combat buggy.

From there, it was a simple case of breaking in to the weapons locker.

Fortunately for Wilda, her old friend Henry had taught her the intricacies of the electrical systems that powered Sakkin's combat equipment. The capacitor that provided electricity was hidden under the chassis in an armored case. She popped the emergency release and unclipped the thermos sized device from its housing.

Depending on its level of charge the capacitor held enough energy to power a village for weeks. It was also the key to the weapons locker.

She found a power tether at the rear of the CPV. The spool of cable was designed to power another vehicle in the event of a capacitor failure. She stripped the cable exposing the wiring. Holding the capacitor at the base she briefly touched its contacts to the tether.

There was a sharp crack, and acrid smoke filled the air as she made directly for the locker that housed emergency equipment. The blast of electric energy had fried the digital lock, allowing her to pry it open. Inside she found a submachine railer and a combat vest laden with the tools of her trade: explosive charges, plasma grenades, and a carbon nano-tube blade.

The equipment was meant as an emergency stash for a Sakkin operative. Wilda enjoyed the irony that it was arming an enemy. Donning the gear she considered climbing back to the vent. Given it was already weakened, she doubted it would hold the extra weight of her gear. It was probably less risky to cause a diversion and slip back into the facility to target the power plant.

Her vest contained two programmable explosive charges. She'd use one as a distraction and the other to target the power plant. She slapped the charge on a rusted pickup parked in the rack closest to the damaged garage door. Then she snuck behind the other vehicles until she reached the far corner. The two mechops guarding the breach were focused outward. Behind them, maintenance technicians and their robots were unloading equipment from an elevator.

She waited for them to finish then triggered the charge. The explosion tossed the pickup out of the rack into the mechops. Sprinting for the elevator she saw that the doors were closing and dived inside.

"What the hell," snapped a technician. "Who are you?"

"Open the doors on the next level," she replied as they rose.

He fell silent and punched the appropriate button. When the doors opened, Wilda raised her weapon and stepped into the corridor. Symbols on the walls warned of the presence of toxins, radiation, and flammable liquids. She was in the right place.

Chapter Eleven

Bismarck Facility, Eastern Turkey

Crispy felt the explosion as he was searching the accommodation wing of the facility. Eight Two wasn't showing up on the CCTV network or biometric tracking system.

"Explosion on the garage level. A tech is reporting that she exited on the engineering level. I'm deploying wasp drones," transmitted Yitzhak, from the operations room. "Live streaming now."

His shifters stepped in behind him as his bionic eyeball displayed a live feed from the tiny wasp drones. They raced through an access pipe and exited into the corridor on the engineering level.

As he entered the elevator the drones found his target and painted her with a flashing red designator. He caught a glimpse of her face as she turned and raised a weapon. Then the feed died. She had destroyed the drones.

"She's armed," transmitted Yitzhak. "Capture order has been augmented with kill."

Crispy smirked as the elevator dropped. He'd just been given the green light to put a railer slug in Eight Two's brain. "Two up. Shoot to kill," he ordered his shifters. "Adopt adaptive camouflage profile." He hit the transmit button on his weapon. "Power off."

Wilda wasn't surprised when the engineering section was plunged into darkness. The wasp drones she'd destroyed had revealed her position and now Sakkin cronies were coming to try and kill her.

Cradling her railer she waited for her vision to adjust to the gloom. She was fortunate that the power plant's screens were still active. If the screens had turned off, even her enhanced eyes would have been sightless. The interior of the engineering level was now shades of grey.

She found the door to the power plant and shot out the lock with her railer. Entering, her ears were assaulted by a humming that seemed to reverberate through her entire body. The fusion reactor was not one she'd seen before. It looked older than the ones at the *Institute*. As big as four shipping containers, it sat in the center of the room surrounded by piping, walkways and cables.

She'd received training in sabotage at the *Institute*. They'd been taught to find the weak point of the system, the lynchpin that held everything together. In the case of a reactor, it was the cooling fluid. Without it, the core would quickly overheat and meltdown, causing irreparable damage and a terminal shut down. It would render the fusion core utterly useless and shut off the outflow of toxic chemicals and radiation.

There was a pair of steel pipes on the far side of the reactor. She laid a hand on each. One of them was icy cold, the other warm. Taking her final explosive charge from her combat vest she detached the firing remote and armed the bomb. She knelt and slapped it on the cold-water intake.

As she rose she caught a glimpse of movement at a far corner of the reactor. A shadow flashed toward her at unbelievable speed. It was one of the clankers that had abducted her from the Barzani. Bringing her railer to bear she fired a penetrator directly into the machine.

The high-velocity slug tore through it with an ear-splitting crack. It shimmered, and she could make out the detail of its humanoid body as it descended upon her. She fired the railer again. This time the round tore through the mechop's head smashing through the nanotech coating and pulverizing the electronics within. Wilda expected the machine to drop, but it kept on coming, headless, limbs outstretched.

Rolling underneath the inlet piping she narrowly avoided the robot's attempt to grab her. The machine dropped to its knees and thrust its arms in after her. Her railer hissed twice, and tungsten penetrators tore through its torso. It crashed to the ground in a sparking heap.

Steam hissed from somewhere behind it, and an alarm wailed as she crawled under the pipes, away from the shattered robot. There was a clang from above as another of the mechops hunted her.

She knew why they weren't shooting. They were trying to avoid damaging the reactor. Rolling out from under the pipes she rose to a knee and aimed her railer. Before she could fire, it was ripped from her hands.

The mechop grabbed her arm in a clamp-like grip and yanked her from the floor. Twisting her body she narrowly avoided the punch it aimed at her torso. Her right hand found the carbon bladed dagger in her vest, and she rammed it into the machine's shoulder joint.

The limb died, releasing her from its grip. Hitting the ground she rolled then sprung from the floor into the corner of the room. She ran the wall and leaped for the relative safety of the railing above. Grasping the rungs she flipped onto the walkway that ran over the generator equipment.

The move had taken her less than a second, but it was enough time for the agile mechop to recover and give chase. It leaped from the floor and landed on the walkway behind her. Wilda turned, slipped a grenade from its pouch and twisted off the safety bail. She let the trigger activate and counted down the seconds as she ran. She turned her head at three seconds and lobbed the grenade as she dove from the gangway.

The mechop wore the full blast of the bomb and was blown rearward like a rag doll. A hunk of shrapnel slammed into Wilda's armor, and splinters peppered her legs and arms as she hit the floor with a thump. Ears ringing she staggered to her feet and limped toward the generator room exit.

As she approached, the siren changed in pitch, and an orange light flashed through the smoke and steam. There was an armored figure standing on the other side of the heavy glass door, Crispy.

There was an ever so slight smile on his scarred face. "Now you burn," he mouthed.

Three floors above the reactor, Yitzhak was watching Eight Two via one of the many cameras in the engineering sector.

He had the feed on the primary screen so Marnisha Copeland could see the fate of her creation.

"What's going on in there?" she asked.

"Her railer slug penetrated the reactor core. She's currently being bombarded by radiation."

"Can you get her out of there?"

He grunted. "Once she's been incapacitated. Did you see what she did to the mechops?"

"The radiation could kill her."

"Once she's down, I'll send in a medop, and we'll get her straight to the infirmary. We've got all the necessary equipment to treat radiation poisoning. Then she'll be handed over to the rendition team." He glanced at another screen, which showed the progress of an aircraft. It had commenced its approach profile.

"How long is this going to take?"

"An average human can withstand 500 rads worth of exposure before collapsing, but she isn't average, is she?"

"Are we in danger here?"

Yitzhak shook his head. "The leak is localized and contained. I can shut down the reactor and complete repairs in less than an hour. It might take a few more minutes for her to drop."

Copeland's eyes had never left the screen where Eight Two was standing facing the doorway. The high definition feed showed every detail of her face, and the sweat beading on her forehead.

Suddenly the girl raised her hands toward the glass door. Her left hand formed a fist, and she raised the middle finger in a defiant salute. Then she depressed the trigger that she was holding.

The video feed went blank as an explosion sent tremors through the building.

"What the hell was that?" Copeland asked as alarms wailed, lights flashed, and an engineering interface replaced the video on the central screen.

"That suicidal bitch just blew the fucking coolant intakes. We're going to lose the reactor!" he screamed.

"Do I need to evacuate?" she asked.

"We all need to fucking evacuate."

Crispy pushed his face against the door in an attempt to see into the devastated reactor room. Smoke and debris swirled against the heavy glass, completely obscuring the interior.

"We've lost the reactor. All personnel and essential equipment are being moved to the roof for evacuation," transmitted Yitzhak. "We're abandoning ship."

"That bitch is still in there," he snapped, turning his back on the reactor and striding down the corridor. Behind him, heavy metal doors slid shut, sealing the area.

"The radiation level is off the charts. If she wasn't killed by the blast, she's going to be fried. The reactor will burn out, but not for a day or two. It's getting zero water. We've only got six hours of power in the capacitors." He paused. "Bismarck is done. At least for now."

Crispy felt something as he strode away from the reactor room toward the elevators. He wasn't exactly sure what it was. His mission to neutralize Eight Two was complete, he was redeemed. Yet he felt empty, almost as if he had lost something. Shaking the thought, he entered the elevator and made his way to the operations room.

Marnisha Copeland and Yitzhak were the only personnel inside. The facility's remaining crew would already be on the hangar deck.

"We can fit our non-combatants on your vertjet," said Yitzhak. "The rest of us will evacuate with the rendition team."

Copeland gestured to the equipment in the room. "And all this?"

"I've messaged the Director. It will be his decision on whether we lock it down or destroy it. Crispy, I need you to escort Director Copeland up to the deck. Her aircraft is in a holding pattern and will land once you're in position."

An incoming call sounded, and Yitzhak touched his tablet. The face that appeared on screen was one that Crispy recognized immediately, Leon Wilkens. His aircraft was within transmission range.

"Yitzhak, have you and Crispy secured Eight two?"

Copeland paused at the door to listen.

"Not exactly. She was killed sabotaging this facility's power plant," replied Yitzhak.

"You have a body?"

"We will once we've decontaminated the reactor room and sifted through the damage. In the meantime, I'm requesting your assistance in evacuating personnel to Incirlik."

On-screen Wilkens nodded. "My aircraft will be at your disposal. I'll see you soon."

Copeland stepped out of the room and strode toward the elevator. Crispy followed her and stood quietly in the corner. Her aircraft was waiting when they exited the landing hangar. She strode past the waiting non-combatant personnel and disappeared inside the sleek vertjet.

"The rest of you can board," Crispy ordered.

The fifteen Sumsunto workers were the last of the civilians at Bismarck. The personnel that remained, less than a dozen, were all security officers or weapon techs. Crispy watched as the vertjet lifted off and accelerated away. As his eyes tracked the aircraft he spotted the inbound flight. Larger and boxier the military vertjet seemed to lumber across the sky.

He waited as it slowed, engines rotating to provide downward thrust, and finally touched down on the battle-scarred landing pad. When the ramp dropped, Leon Wilkens, wearing a lightweight exoskeleton, was the first to appear. "Crispy, you kill that bitch?" he asked as a fourganic squad exited the aircraft.

He nodded. "We cornered her in the reactor room."

"Do we know what she was doing here?" Wilkens asked as they entered the hangar.

"She joined a local militia. They launched an attack on the facility."

"Traitorous bitch."

The elevator opened, and Yitzhak appeared. "Who the fuck are these amateurs?" he joked.

"Yitzhak, you old dog. How long has it been?"

The men embraced.

"Over fifteen years," replied Yitzhak. "But, the good news is we'll be working together from here on in. I just received a message from Director Lerner. He's sending additional resources to deal with this insurrection. You and your team have been allocated to the mission. Together we're going to hunt down and wipe out the Barzani rebels."

Turkey-Kurdistan Border Region

Wilda clung to the side of a boulder as the raging torrent of the river tugged at her. She fought to keep her head above water. The icy cold river was leeching her energy as she struggled to stay afloat. Drawing on every ounce of her strength she managed to haul herself out of the river and onto the rocky bank.

Rolling onto her side she plunged her fingers into her throat and vomited the contents of her stomach. During her escape from the reactor she'd swallowed mouthfuls of toxic, irradiated water; water, that if absorbed into her system, could kill her.

She vomited again and again until she was dry retching. Then, wiping her mouth with her wet sleeve, she staggered to her feet. She had no way of knowing whether purging the water would save her. She may have already ingested a lethal dose of radiation.

Her charge had blown apart the reactor's cooling system exposing the waste outlet, giving her an exit from the building. She'd had to abandon her vest and weapon to fit inside the pipe, and even then, it had been tight. The outlet had run for less than a dozen yards before dropping her directly into the river. From there, the current had swept her downstream through a series of rapids.

Drenched to the bone and with nightfall only hours away, Wilda knew she needed to find shelter and start a fire. She guessed she was less than five miles downstream from Bismarck. That meant the abandoned village she'd discovered previously wasn't far away, and the walk would help warm her.

As she followed the river, she took the time to process the last twelve hours. She'd gone from thinking she'd found her home village to learning that she'd been grown in a machine. Remembering the proximity drive, she checked her pockets and pulled it out. Somehow the coin-sized data module had remained with her despite the fury of the attack in the reactor room and the white water. She wondered if the radiation might have damaged the data itself.

The tiny device held the answers as to who she really was. She contemplated tossing it into the river. Whatever information it contained would make no difference to her now.

But, something in the back of her mind told her to hang on to it. She slipped it back into her pocket as she spotted the burial ground of the abandoned village.

The walk had dried her somewhat, but the sun was close to falling behind the mountains. If she couldn't make a fire it was going to be a rough night.

The village had been eerie the previous time she'd been here. It was worse now. Her radiation poisoning was impacting her grasp on reality. Every shadow was someone watching her, or worse still, one of the shapeshifting mechops that had almost killed her.

Still, she managed to gather a pile of dried wood and construct a fire bow from a piece of cord and a branch. After a few furious minutes she managed to generate enough friction to bring an ember to life. Tipping it into dry grass, her breath coaxed a tiny flickering flame and she finally had a small fire.

When she'd warmed a little she searched the nearby huts and found a dusty blanket. Exhausted, she fell into a deep dreamless sleep.

A sharp pain in her right leg woke her with a start. She opened her eyes and found herself staring into the muzzle of a rifle.

"Get up," a voice growled.

Incirlik, Turkey

Marnisha Copeland waited for the evacuees from Bismarck to disembark her jet, before stepping out onto the tarmac of the former US Air Force base at Incirlik.

Now a Sakkin facility, the airbase was a hive of activity. A massive aerostat, the Jericho, was tethered on a landing pad and surrounded by cargo vehicles laden with equipment. The airship was a floating special operations support base. Flying well beyond the range of heavy weapons, it provided small teams with communications, fire support, intelligence and a deployment platform.

"Beautiful, isn't she."

Copeland wasn't surprised to find Avi Lerner at the base. She turned to face the handsome director who'd stepped out of an electric utility vehicle.

"A large bag filled with gas and bristling with weapons. Beautiful is not exactly the word I would use to describe it, but yes, it is impressive."

"I heard there were some problems at Bismarck?"

"Yes, it would seem that your people stirred up an ant nest."

"Really, I heard it was one of yours."

Copeland shrugged. "You can't blame one teenage girl for destroying an entire base."

He smirked. "Hardly destroyed. We'll have it back to full operational status in no time. And, now that your problem child has illuminated the key threat group in the area, we can focus our attention on eliminating them. Oh, and I was sorry to hear that she perished during her little rampage. I was looking forward to meeting her."

Copeland's watch pinged, informing her that the vertjet had been refueled.

"Good luck with your operation, Avi. I've got to get back to Cape Town."

Leaving him on the tarmac, she took her seat in the aircraft. As the door closed and the autonomous system went through its preflight checks, she gazed out the window at the airship and the masses of military hardware being prepared. If she had her way, it would all be scrapped, and the money poured into her programs. If there was one thing that Wilda had proved, in her short life, it was that quality could generate effects far beyond quantity.

Bismarck Facility, Eastern Turkey

Crispy watched from the safety of a radiation-proof exoskeleton as engineering mechops lifted slabs of concrete and pieces of metal. He'd already searched the entire reactor room for Wilda's body but had failed to find it. She had to be under the debris of the blown water intakes.

As he waited he glanced at the control panel for the reactor. Wilda's sabotage had slagged the ancient plant. Without cooling water its fail-safes had triggered, collapsing the core onto itself, and turning the thousand-ton fusion plant into a useless hunk of radiated metal. Engineers had estimated it would take months to remove it and install a more modern unit.

"They've found something," announced Yitzhak over the comms link.

Crispy made his way to the corner and moved past the mechops, who stood waiting. There, below the shattered outlet pipe, in an inch of irradiated water, lay a combat vest and a battered submachine railer.

"She's not here. She must have escaped through the outlet pipe."

"Damn it," said Yitzhak.

"You think she's still alive? Wouldn't the radiation have killed her?"

"No. You ganics can endure radiation levels that would kill an average human. She's probably sick, but she'll heal. That's if she didn't drown in the river."

"We should deploy drones."

"We don't have the assets until we're reinforced. When that happens, our priority is to hunt the Barzani leaders. Eight Two, if she's alive, will have to wait."

Crispy punched the reactor wall in frustration.

"Steady, boy," snapped Yitzhak. "We'll find her, eventually."

Chapter Twelve

Turkey-Kurdistan Border Region

Every drop of water hitting the stone floor of her cell echoed through Wilda's head like it was being slammed with a hammer. Her body trembled and sweat drenched her clothes as she huddled on a thin mattress that had been tossed on the floor. Her every joint ached along with her head as she convulsed.

It was clear to Wilda that she had radiation poisoning from both the reactor and the river water. She knew the symptoms from her training, but had no idea how sick she really was.

The door to her cell creaked open, and she glanced up to see Masrour standing in the opening.

"So the river brought you back to us," he announced as he entered. "And it looks as if you have drunk your own poison." He took what looked to be a small communicator from his pocket and waved it a few inches over her body. It made a soft beeping noise as he examined the screen. Slipping it back into his jacket he took out a canister of pills and dropped them onto the mattress.

"Take these, they'll make you feel better. Tonight, you will face a tribunal that will decide if you are guilty of spying. Although, no matter what the ruling, you may have already been given a death sentence. Take the iodine. I will come back for you in a few hours."

Wilda reached for the pills with a shaking hand and managed to remove the lid. Masrour left, and the cell door clanged shut.

Tiny red pills spilled across the floor. She managed to scoop two into her mouth. They were bitter on her tongue. Swallowing them dry she struggled not to vomit. Then she collapsed onto the mattress and passed out.

The rattle of her cell door woke Wilda with a start. She sat up on the mattress and noted that her joints no longer hurt, and she'd stopped sweating. She wondered if it was the iodine tablets, or maybe her dose of radiation hadn't been as bad as she thought.

A pair of handcuffs hit the ground with a clatter, and a hard-looking Barzani soldier stood in the doorway.

"Put them on."

She snapped the cold steel cuffs onto her wrists.

"This way."

On her way in, she'd been too sick to take in her surroundings. As the soldier escorted her along a dimly lit tunnel she realized they were underground in what looked to be a mine.

She was led out of the tunnel into a brightly lit cavern where vehicles and equipment were parked. Groups of disheveled fighters watched her through cold eyes as she was led past them into a command center.

There were blank screens on all sides of the room and a central table with men seated around it. Masrour was sitting at the head with his lieutenant to his right.

"Bring her here." The commander gestured to a chair a short distance from the table.

The guard pushed her into it, and she sat facing eight stern faces.

"Wilda, you have been accused of spying for Sakkin and deliberately providing false information resulting in the death of twenty two Barzani soldiers. This military tribunal will review the information on hand and determine whether or not you are guilty. Do you understand this?"

She shook her head. "I'm not a spy."

"She understands. I will outline the facts, and then we will pass judgement."

It took the Barzani commander less than twenty minutes to brief his subordinates of the chain of events that had led to their defeat at Bismarck. As he spoke, Wilda's heart sank. Having been a prisoner inside the facility, she had not witnessed the counter-attack by the marauders and Crispy's mechops. The Barzani never actually had a chance of winning.

"Does the accused have anything to add before the tribunal votes?"

Wilda knew that nothing she could say would change the decision that every man at the table had already made. They had been dealt a devastating blow, and someone had to pay the price. "I destroyed the reactor inside Bismarck," she stated calmly. "No longer will it spew death into the river and poison your lands. The Sakkin forces may not have been defeated, but your attack did not fail."

"She's lying," shouted one of the men. "She's a spy lying to save her neck."

Masrour held up his hand, silencing the man. "Yes, but she could also be telling the truth. We can test the water for radiation. If what she says is true, then it will affect our judgment. Return her to the cells."

The guard gestured for Wilda to leave the room. On her way out, she locked eyes with Masrour. He showed no emotion as she stepped into the tunnel.

Her life hung by a thread now. If the damaged reactor had not shut down, there was a good chance it was still leaking radiation and toxins into the river. If that was the case, the Barzani would put her to death.

The two days it took for Masrour and his men to check her claims had allowed Wilda to rest and recover. They'd brought her simple food, clean water and a blanket, then left her to her thoughts. She felt like a prisoner on death row. If they found even a trace of radiation in the river, there was every chance she'd be executed.

She'd managed to sleep, but her dreams no longer included her mother or their village. It was almost as if her subconscious had acknowledged that it was all a fabrication. Instead, her dreams were filled with Behdin, Xeyal and Henry. They were her family, but she could never return to them out of fear that Sakkin would destroy Pendro. Even if the Barzani released her, she would have nowhere to go.

When the door rattled, she'd been ready to strike. Her plan was to incapacitate the guard, steal his jacket and find a way out of the mine. Then she would escape Barzani territory and find a place to lay low.

It wasn't a guard who came for her. It was Masrour. The chief stood in the doorway with her backpack in one hand and a tablet in the other. "It would seem that you have done what we could not."

Wilda rose. "What happens now?"

"There is a war coming and Pendro will need warriors."

"I can't go back. Sakkin will come for me. It will put the entire village in jeopardy."

He shook his head, a sad look in his eyes. "They're coming for everyone, Wilda." He passed her the tablet.

On screen was a map with points marked. She immediately recognized Pendro, Harkanass and Barzani territory. Bismarck was located almost central in the cluster of dots.

"Those dots mark locations for possible mines. Sakkin will push people out of their villages to give the corporations access. If we don't fight back we will lose our lands and our people will die." He took the tablet and offered her backpack. "Come with me."

She took the bag. The weight told her it was full of supplies she would need for her journey. Following him out of the cell he led her to the main cavern.

"Sakkin will come for us, but this time we will be ready."

As the rocky passage opened up, Wilda noticed men working in pairs carrying black equipment cases deeper into the mines. Near the mine opening Wilda was surprised to see an aircraft parked under an old equipment shed. It looked like the predecessor to Sakkin's vertjets, with giant rotors instead of ion thrusters.

Men were unloading more of the cases under the watch of a figure dressed in modern combat armor with a railer slung across his back.

The man turned, and Wilda saw he was young, not much older than her. His chiseled jaw was set with determination, and his dark eyes burned with intensity. He looked like a formidable warrior. There was a familiarity about him that she found almost unnerving.

"Who is that?" asked Wilda as they passed the aircraft and made their way through the mine workshops.

"A new friend. Someone helping us to fight Sakkin. Speaking of friends, one of the reasons I was able to convince the tribunal to acquit you of spying is because someone came looking for you."

They left the mine under a covered walkway that ran a hundred yards into a warehouse. The level of camouflage and deception that the Barzani were employing to evade Sakkin detection was impressive. Coupled with new weaponry, it might even give them the edge required to survive.

They finally emerged into the sunlight, and Wilda savored the warmth on her face. Masrour led her across a street and stopped in front of a coffee house. "We could use your help here Wilda."

"My place is with my family."

"I agree. Soon I will send men to Pendro. You will work with them to prepare your militia. With Barzani support they will be a formidable element in our war against Sakkin. But, till then, rest and spend time with your people." Masrour grasped her hand in a firm grip. "Your friend is inside." With those words, he left her, returning to the tunnels and his preparation for war.

Wilda already knew who would be inside waiting for her, Behdin. The teenager had a knack for getting her out of trouble.

A bell jingled as she pushed open the door, and the rich

scent of roasting coffee hit her nose. She glanced around the small room, searching for Behdin. But the person waiting for her wasn't him.

"Wilda," exclaimed Palin. The young man rose from the table where he was sitting. "I was worried you'd been taken by the marauders."

There were dark bags under the young militia leader's eyes, a scratch on his cheek and his clothing was dusty.

"How did you find me?" she asked.

"After you went missing, I ordered the men to stay in Harkanass, and I followed your tracks. I arrived at the Barzani border yesterday." He lowered his voice. "They're more than a little suspicious of outsiders. But they know my mother and that guy Masrour recognized me."

Wilda was overcome with emotion and wrapped her arms around him, tears streaming from her eyes. "Thank you, thank you so much."

He tentatively returned the hug. "You saved our lives in Harkanass," he said softly. "You will always be a part of our tribe and family. Plus, do you know what my mother would do to me if I didn't bring you home."

They broke and Wilda wiped her cheeks on her sleeve. He picked up his pack and rifle from the corner of the room. "Now, we better get going. The Barzani will take us to their borders, but it's a long walk from there."

Wilda smiled as she shouldered her own bag. "I can't wait to get home."

Sakkin HQ, Capetown Enclave

Marnisha Copeland's aircraft had commenced its approach profile when her watch vibrated, indicating she'd received a priority message.

Checking the screen she noted it was from Lisker, demanding an update. Exhaling, she gathered her thoughts and considered how best to frame the loss of test subject Eight Two. It wasn't a significant setback, but it did amount to a large sum of investment. Fortunately, Eight Two's implant had uploaded when she was detained, providing Copeland with a large amount of data to interrogate.

The vertjet touched down, and she grabbed her bag from one of the seats. The first thing she was going to do was shower. Then she would make an appointment to update the chairman in person.

She never got the chance. Having crossed the bustling air terminal, she entered the VIP lounge and saw that Lisker was sitting on a couch reading from a tablet.

"Hello Marnisha, I trust you had a comfortable trip." His eyes remained focused on the tablet until he'd finished speaking. Then he glanced up with a questioning look on his face.

"Better than some," she replied with a grim smile. "I trust you've been updated on the Bismarck fiasco."

"Yes, Avi made it perfectly clear who he thought was responsible."

"Manfred, that's not fair. When we developed this plan, I had no idea that we'd be transitioning the facility for security operations. It was supposed to have been redundant."

He shrugged. "Situations change, plans adapt. I don't see this as a significant setback. The reactor at Bismarck was poisoning the local river system and needed replacing.

Given it is no longer operational, the locals may refrain from attacking again."

"You don't think mining operations are going to trigger a violent response?"

"No doubt, but we will be adequately prepared. Now, talk to me about the Nemesis program."

"I assure you that the loss of Eight Two will not have an impact. I was able to—"

"Loss? It's my understanding that she successfully escaped the reactor room. Avi was particularly enraged to not find a body."

She managed a smile. "Well, that is good news. I was able to recover the proximity drive. So that component of the program remains intact."

"And the cloning?"

"With the additional data I've gathered from her profile, I'm confident that the next prototypes will have all of her strengths and none of her weaknesses."

"You mean they'll respond to orders and not develop a conscience?"

"Exactly."

"When will they be ready?" He rose from the couch, folded the tablet, and slipped it into his suit jacket.

"They will birth in seventy-five days and be transferred to an accelerated growth program. You can expect them to enter the *Institute* in a little over a year."

Manfred shook his head in amazement. "How many units?"

"Thirty, there will be thirty units available for operations within three years."

Pendro, Kurdistan

Wilda could hear a strange noise over the crunch of gravel under the electric truck's off-road tires. It sounded like fire crackling through dry brush.

It wasn't until the truck came to a halt that she heard cheers and identified the noise, clapping. When the truck's canvas cover was lifted, she saw the entire village had turned out to welcome the militia home.

She let the others climb down from the truck and waited for them to reach their families. The crowd moved toward the town square, where there would be feasting and speeches. Slipping through the window in the back of the cabin she exited through the passenger side door.

Heading away from the celebrations she made a beeline for Behdin and Xeyal's house. She hadn't gone fifty yards when she almost ran into the pair coming the other way.

"Wilda!" screamed Xeyal, launching herself into Wilda's arms. "I knew you'd come back."

Behdin joined the hug as Henry, the dog, jumped up on her leg. She was overcome with a sense of belonging as the pair held her tight. Then, when they broke, she knelt and scooped her dog into her arms. The little brown hound showered her with kisses as the siblings bombarded her with questions.

"Were you at the battle of Harkanass?" asked Behdin.

"I was there," she murmured, burying her face in the dog's soft ears.

"I heard our militia fought back and defeated the marauders," Behdin exclaimed.

"They fought well."

"No, you did," Palin said. He'd followed Wilda from the truck. "And the entire village needs to know."

Wilda gave the dog's ears a ruffle, and rose to face the chief's son. "Palin, the victory at Harkanass is the militia's. No one benefits from anyone thinking differently."

He frowned. "I will respect your wishes, but I will never forget what you did. We would have been killed if it wasn't for you."

She reached out and grasped his shoulder. "You found me, Palin. The score is even."

He smiled. "You should all join the celebrations."

"We'll be there in a minute."

Palin left them, walking quickly away. When he was out of earshot, Behdin spoke. "What did you do at Harkanass?"

"Nothing special. The important thing is I came back and…" She reached out and put an arm around each of them. "I'm not leaving again."

Wilda ran through a field with her hair dancing in the warm air. Henry, ears and tongue flapping, was hot on her heels, letting out excited yaps.

Reaching the bottom of a steep rocky slope she paused and turned to wait for the others. Palin, Behdin and Xeyal were spread out across the field, as they gave chase.

The chief's son was first to arrive. Breathing heavily he braced his arms on his thighs, letting out a groan.

Xeyal and Behdin were hot on his heels and joined them a moment later. Like Palin, they were short on breath and fighting for oxygen.

Wilda, composed with only the slightest elevation in heart rate, gave them thirty seconds rest before taking off up the slope at a sprint. She climbed a few hundred yards in no time, reaching her favorite rocky outcrop. This time even Henry struggled, the dog arriving seconds after her.

Palin, Behdin and Xeyal reached the giant slab of rock within seconds of each other. It was a weekly ritual that had started with a bet. Palin, having been subsequently beaten by Wilda, had suggested they complete the two-mile dash at least once a week. Now, three months on, they'd all improved their times, but still, no one could beat Wilda.

"I don't think I'll ever get tired of that view," said Palin between breaths.

The outcrop was high above the valley floor and gave them spectacular views across the river, fields and the village where it butted up against cliffs opposite.

"This is home for me now," said Wilda as she sat. Henry leaned against her, tongue lolling.

The four youths sat in silence.

After a moment, Xeyal asked a question. "Do you think the robots will ever come back?"

"If they do," said Palin. "We will be ready for them, won't we, Wilda."

"We will be ready," echoed Wilda. The words rolled off her tongue with ease, but deep down, she knew it was far from the truth. Sakkin had weapons and capabilities beyond anything that the village militia could handle. Pendro would need powerful allies. Allies like Masrour and the Barzani.

When Sakkin came, they would secure the northern escape routes and then sweep in from the south. There were suitable landing zones and unobstructed approaches where berserkers could lay down heavy fire. Anyone attempting to flee would be forced into the mountains where they could be targeted by drones or picked up by mechops. Then, clear of any resistance, the mining would begin.

Wilda exhaled and attempted to push the thoughts from

her mind. She didn't want to have to think of infiltration routes and cut off locations. She had the garden to prepare for spring planting.

She touched the leather pouch that hung from her neck and grasped it in her hand. Inside it was the drive that contained the programming Sakkin had used to create her. She couldn't change her past, but she could write her future and here, in the village of Pendro, was where she was going to do it.

More from Jack Silkstone

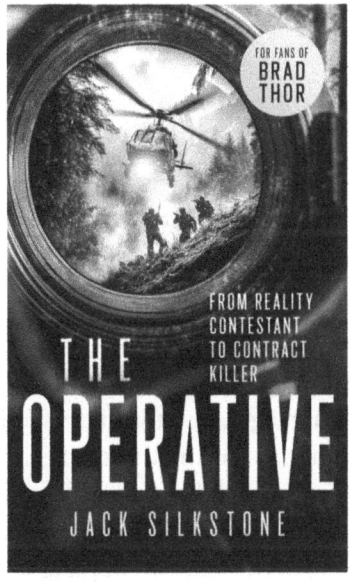

vinci-books.com/silkstone-operative

Fame is the perfect cover, but in this game, survival is the ultimate prize.

Unsuspecting reality TV contestants are thrust into a shadowy world of espionage. As they compete for stardom, a covert organisation molds them into unwitting agents, exploiting their ambition for evil purposes. With the contestants blackmailed and trapped, the line between reality and deception blur. Who will survive the ultimate reality TV show and what dark turn will victory take?

Turn the page for a free preview...

The Operative: Prologue

He was a ghost, a highly trained operative with multiple identities, three languages, and two dozen confirmed kills. A man you didn't want to meet in a dark alley.

His latest mission didn't look at all challenging. The target was a middle-aged man living in the Australian city of Melbourne. In twelve years of working for the company, he'd taken three jobs in the land down under. It was a favored retirement destination for intelligence types. It was probably because it was miles from anywhere, but, as his kill count revealed, it wasn't far enough.

He checked his device and reread the short bio. Brian Schofield was fifty-six years old and in average shape, judging by the photo. There was a wife and a kid. Not a problem, murder-suicides were his specialty.

There was no historical data, not that it mattered. He wasn't here to pass judgment, only execute the sentence.

"Damien Broader, your vehicle is ready."

He glanced up at the hire car sales desk and saw the female attendant was holding an envelope. Slipping the phone into his pocket, he shouldered his backpack and went to the counter. Taking the envelope, he thanked her and exited the office. It took him less than a minute to find the allocated vehicle and throw his bag on the passenger seat.

It was a short drive from the airport to the suburb where his target lived. The streets were wide and tree-lined with open gardens that suggested minimal crime, an excellent place to raise a family.

He'd used a burner account to book an apartment nearby and planned to commence his recon that evening. Experience told him he wouldn't need to hang around. Most people's weekday routine was consistent. He'd check it out tonight, procure the required equipment, and do the job the following day. He'd be on a flight out before the bodies were cold.

The phone in his pocket vibrated as he pulled into the space allocated to his apartment. Killing the engine, he checked the screen. A single phrase appeared in his notifications.

Data has been corrupted.

It took a split second for the gravity of the situation to hit home. He tried logging into the secure application and confirmed that it was down. The system stored nothing locally. The phone was now a brick. He used a cloth to wipe his prints from the device and tossed it in the footwell. The sim was a burner purchased through a cut-out. Nothing, not the car or the apartment, could be traced. It was all expendable.

He grabbed his bag, left the vehicle, and walked onto the street. He was on his own now, burnt.

As he made his way to a main road to flag a taxi, his

earlier confidence evaporated. Mission forgotten, his only thought was survival. He needed to get out of Australia, and fast.

A passing taxi stopped, and he directed the driver to the international airport. He had a flexible airfare booked under a contingency ID. Exhaling, he reassured himself that his procedures were flawless. *The Entity* may have had a compromise, but the now bricked phone was his only link to them. He was clean.

By the time he was moving through the crowded departures concourse, he was back to his calm self. At the business class check-in, the attendant handed him his ticket with a smile.

"Alan Crete." The voice behind him was firm with an icy edge.

He hadn't heard his real name spoken out loud in almost a decade. Turning, he found himself face to face with a broad-shouldered, stern-faced man in a tailored suit. Backing him up were five similarly dressed men. His trained eye spotted the tell-tale bulge of a pistol on the hip of each of them.

"This is the end of the road."

Alan moved quickly, palming the man in the face and smashing his nose. At the same time, he threw an arm over his shoulder and spun him into a headlock.

As he went for the man's pistol, the others moved as fast as he had. The last thing the assassin ever saw was a pistol muzzle. A security officer's bullet punched a neat hole in his forehead and expanded inside his brain, killing him instantly. He dropped to the ground behind the officer he'd assaulted.

"Cordon off the area," the man croaked. "Don't let anyone near the body."

The Operative: Chapter One

David Martin stepped out of his rental SUV and squinted as he donned a pair of designer sunglasses. Dough-faced with curly black hair, he was an unremarkable-looking man with an unimpressive physique. At first glance, most people assumed he was an accountant or, worse, a real estate agent. In fact, he was a lawyer and fixer for a shadowy intelligence consultancy known as *The Entity*.

It wasn't his first trip to Texas, and he wasn't thrilled to be so far from the safety of the urban environment. This place is a dusty shit hole, he thought as he slammed the car door and surveyed his surroundings.

The Delta Ranch, such a lame name, he thought. It was smack bang in the middle of nowhere surrounded by thousands of acres of rugged, tree-covered hills. He imagined that they were crawling with rattlesnakes and spiders.

The ranch house was a short walk, but that wasn't where he'd find who he was looking for. Instead, he made for a sizeable open-ended barn, where boots poked out from under a tractor.

"X, is that you?" he asked between bursts of a rattle gun.

A leathery face appeared from under the machinery.

"Do I look like that behemoth? He's out back." The man gestured through the barn then slid back under the tractor.

"Thanks," mumbled David as he straightened his sports jacket and entered the barn, careful not to get horse shit on his loafers.

The structure had stalls on both sides and an open door at the back through which he could hear the crack of gunfire. Exiting, David made his way to an open area cleared between two low hills.

He spotted the man he was looking for crouched over a hefty tractor tire.

X, a massive lantern-jawed former CIA paramilitary officer, let out a grunt as he flipped the tire. Before it dropped, he sprinted toward a row of steel targets, unslinging the carbine that hung across his back as he moved.

Skidding to a halt, he rapidly engaged the targets in one direction, changed magazines then hit them in reverse before unloading. He slung the weapon across his back as he strode toward David.

"What's up?" his said, deep and abrupt.

David noted that despite the grey at his temples and the wrinkles on his face, the retired paramilitary officer looked as fit, if not fitter, than ever.

"Good to see you too."

"Niceties are for nice people. We ain't fucking nice!" X gestured to the barn. "I'm guessing we need to talk somewhere secure?"

"Preferably."

David had known X for nearly a decade and knew the big man wasn't one for small talk, which was OK with him. He followed him back to the barn into one of the horse stalls, lined with cupboards to hold tack. X fished a device from his pocket and waved it over a wall panel. There was a click, and a cabinet slid sideways, revealing stairs that disappeared into a basement.

"Very 007," said David as he followed him down.

Lights flickered on, illuminating a bunker. X strode across to a line of lockers, punched in a code, opened the door, and placed his carbine beside a dozen other weapons.

"Rather well equipped," said David as he sat on a Chesterfield sofa.

"Beer?"

"Why not."

X grabbed two cold bottles from a fridge, twisted off the caps, and handed one to the lawyer. Then he lowered his hulking frame on to a couch opposite. "So, what have you got?"

"We've had a compromise," said David.

"How bad?"

"Four of our best field operatives."

"And the rest?"

"In hiatus."

"That's untidy."

"To say the least. Which brings me to my next point. We're enacting the plan."

X took a swig from his beer and swallowed. "What plan are you talking about? We had a lot of plans."

David smiled. "Plan Survivor."

X frowned. "No shit! The board approved it?"

"They did, and you and I will run it."

"We got a budget?"

David reached into his jacket and withdrew a folded piece of paper. "This is your contract." He handed it over.

X inspected the document and let out a long whistle. "That's a decent lump of treasure."

The lawyer nodded. "It's a big job. You up for it?"

X finished his beer and wiped his chin. "Ain't got anything else on."

Jennifer Murphy sat in her cubicle on the eleventh floor of an office block in Charlotte, North Carolina. Middle-aged, she had shoulder-length curly brown hair and blue eyes. She was in reasonable shape, training three times a week at a local gym to maintain her figure. She'd described herself on a dating site as bubbly and a chronic oversharer.

Jen, to her friends, was a case manager for a multinational insurance company. A job she loathed, and subsequently, she spent a lot of time planning her holidays. Today, she was researching horse trekking in the Italian Alps.

"Jenny, have you wrapped up that O'Malley case yet?" her supervisor called across the office.

She minimized her internet browser, replacing it with a spreadsheet of her allocated cases, all of which were on schedule. "No, Neville. I'm still waiting on the photos."

Neville spoke from behind her. "Well, get onto it. I need that case cleared by the end of the week."

"They're an older couple, Neville. I'm waiting on their daughter to take better images."

"Jenny, I don't care. Get it done."

As he moved to the next cubicle, she shook her head. "What the hell am I doing?" she murmured as she scanned her case files. Forty years old and working a crappy insurance job to fund holidays, which she went on alone. Not exactly where thirty-year-old her would have hoped to be.

Glancing over her shoulder, she saw Neville had returned to his office. Reopening her browser, she turned her attention back to the horse trek.

In her imagination, she was already there. She was cantering up a flinty hillside between olive-laden trees on a beautiful mare, spurred on by her handsome Italian guide.

Her fantasy was interrupted by a gentle cough. "That doesn't look like work, darling."

Her best friend and work colleague, Ben, leaned over her shoulder. "Does look amazing, though."

"Yeah, I know, and I've almost got enough leave."

"Did you see the email I sent you? I've got a better option."

She opened her email client and found his message. Opening it, she frowned. "What's this?"

"Perfect for you, is what it is. I found it on Facebook and thought Jen has to do this."

The email was a flyer for what looked to be a reality TV show called *The Operative*. She read the Tag Line.

From Zero to Hero. We're taking the average Joe off the street and turning them into James Bond.

"They're looking for people just like you," said Ben.

"You mean ordinary?"

He laughed. "Not ordinary, normal. Come on, babe, you'd crush this. Plus, it would get you out of this boring ass office. Even if it's just for a day to try out."

She opened the application form. "Ben, it's ten pages long. I don't have time for this."

"Of course not. I mean you've got to plan your horse holiday in Italy. So, I've filled out most of it already."

She scrolled down and saw that he'd done exactly that.

"Jen, fill out the gaps and email it in. Come on, what have you got to lose?"

"Fine! But you're buying me a triple-shot caramel latte. It's the only way I will get through the afternoon."

"Deal. You finish the application, and I'll run downstairs to Starbucks. But you better have that application in by the time I return."

He left the office as she started reading the application in detail. The first question asked why she would make the ultimate operative. She took a moment to think before typing her response.

Because no one would ever suspect me.

"Nick, your ex-wife is on line two."

Nick Liu looked up from his laptop and saw the pained expression on his elderly assistant, Magda's, face. "What does she want?"

She shrugged. "Money?"

The American-born Chinese lawyer stared at the flashing light on his desk phone as he exhaled. He'd been divorced for over six months, but the woman wouldn't leave him alone, and he couldn't say no.

"Stop giving that leech money," grumbled his father, the managing partner of the law firm, as he entered the office and dumped an armful of case files on his desk. "I want these annotated by the end of the week."

"Dad, one of the associates can do that."

"I'm not asking one of the associates. I'm asking you."

His father shot him a withering look as he left Nick's office, leaving him with the pile of folders and the flashing phone.

He stared at the light, which seemed to pulse in time with his heartbeat. His palms were sweaty as he picked up the handset and stabbed the call button.

"About time, Nick. That's why you don't have any clients, right? You keep them waiting on the phone all day."

"Anna, what do you want?"

"Want? What do I want? Is that any way to talk to the mother of your child?"

"Anna, it's a dog, not a child. Now look, I'm swamped. Can you tell me what you want?"

"He's not just a dog. It's bad enough that I had to raise him while you were at work. Now you don't want him to get the education he deserves."

"How much?"

"Three thousand dollars."

"Three thousand for dog training," he clenched his teeth. "Fine. I'll transfer it today." He placed the phone back in the cradle and sighed as he wiped his hands on his suit pants. Anna had divorced him to run off with some asshole personal trainer, which crushed his self-esteem. Something she had no problem exploiting at every opportunity.

It wasn't like he was in bad shape. He trained most days, watched what he ate, and tried to get enough sleep. But how was he supposed to compete with a ripped fitness instructor who worked out for a living?

His elderly assistant reappeared in his doorway. "Nick, the printer is broken again."

Well, at least he still had Magda.

"I'm going to have her number blocked," she said as he went to the law firm's common area print station.

"Thanks, Magda, but that's not necessary. Now, what's going on with the printer?"

"It's got some kind of weird glitch."

Nick checked the device's error code and identified a network problem. He opened the server cupboard and inspected the interface. A moment later, he'd rectified the problem.

The printer hummed, confirming the solution.

"If only you were as good with women as you are with computers."

"Wow, thanks Magda."

"This is for you." She thrust a printed page into his hands. "I think you should consider it." He frowned, examining the page as he returned to his desk.

Magda had printed what looked to be a social media post for a reality TV show called *The Operative*. The tagline caught his eye, and he immediately pictured himself dressed in a tuxedo, casually strolling into a casino.

"I thought you might be interested," said Magda from the door.

He laughed. "Magda, it's every balding middle-aged divorcee's fantasy. From Joe Schmo to James Bond."

"Then put in your application. If you're successful, you'll have to take three months leave without a call from that evil ex-wife, which is a holiday for me too. Then, when you win, we can go halves in the five hundred grand."

Nick typed the URL on the paper into his browser and opened the ten-page entry form. "You know what, Magda. I'm going to do it, but if I win, I'm keeping all the cash. My days of handing all my money to women are over."

"So far, we've had over nine thousand entrants. Based on your provided criteria, we've narrowed those down to a base of two hundred." A smartly dressed production consultant, Fiona Yang, gestured to a digital board displaying thousands of mug shots of potential candidates. On cue, most of them faded away, and the remaining hundreds came together into two blocks titled East Coast and West Coast.

David was impressed with the consultant. Two weeks earlier, he'd presented her with the concept documents that he and X had drafted, and already she'd set the ball rolling in precisely the direction he'd envisaged.

"Looks good." He glanced at X.

The former paramilitary officer sat wedged in a sleek white office chair dressed in a fitted suit that barely contained his massive frame. "Do we get the final sign-off?" he asked gruffly.

"Of course," answered Fiona. "I've sent David a link to our secure proprietary website. You will be able to access it easily. From there, you can approve the final hundred contestants for each pre-selection location."

"Excellent," said David.

"I'm excited about this project. It's a unique idea that has the potential to develop a great following. Thanks again for choosing us to help you put it together."

"We're very pleased to have you on the team," replied David. "Now, talk us through the pre-selection."

"Certainly. Again, I've used your direction to shape the program." She gestured to the screen, and the faces were replaced with maps. "I've got east and west coast teams preparing the locations and hiring the necessary crew. We should easily meet the timeline you've put in place. Fortunately, we have a standing relationship with a company we worked with on a similar project."

"What was the project?" asked X.

"Hunt for the Ultimate Ninja. You might have seen it."

"Nah, don't think so."

David hadn't either. He didn't watch television.

"Well, they used a lot of equipment that I think we can employ during the pre-selection. They also ran a fairly comprehensive command center setup we can utilize."

"Very efficient," said David.

"Thank you, the key component we needed to discuss was the budget for each location."

"Yes, what's the number?"

"I'm sorry?"

"How much do you need?"

She chuckled. "That's not usually how it works. I was expecting you to give me a number."

David turned to X, who shrugged. He had no idea what it cost to run something like this, and the board had given him carte blanche. "Funding isn't going to be an issue. Draw up a budget and have it sent to my assistant."

"OK, that's easy." She made a note on her smart device. "Right, next item on the agenda, the selection course. I've reached out to a company in New Zealand that specializes in this style of event. They're in the middle of drafting a concept that aligns with your requirements. I take it you would like me to negotiate the budget?"

"You got it," said David.

She made another note. "That brings us to the director. Have you had a chance to look over the names I put forward?"

David took his phone from his jacket and found Fiona's

email. His assistant had highlighted one of the five names. "Charles Chen looks good."

"I agree, he's done a lot of reality TV and will be a great fit for the project."

"Right, so that's a wrap!" exclaimed David.

"If you're happy, then I'm happy."

David rose and shook her hand before leaving the office.

"That chick's way too switched on," said X once they were in David's SUV.

"I agree. We'll part ways once the selection is over. I've had a background check run on the director. He's not going to be a problem."

"Do we need a director?"

David nodded. "It's essential that the project looks legitimate as long as possible. Don't worry; you will have complete autonomy to run the training how you see fit. Have you selected your team?"

"Yep, they're already at Camp X-Ray."

"X-Ray, isn't that the name of the prison at Guantanamo Bay?"

"Yep."

David looked sideways at the hulking operator. "We're trying to build something here, not destroy their will to live."

X shrugged. "Y'all gotta break 'em down to build 'em up."

"Come up with something more marketable."

"Fine, I'll call it The Ranch."

"Except the locals don't use that term. They call them Stations."

X rolled his eyes. "Fine, let's call it the goddamn Station."

As they left the production company, Fiona remained in

the meeting room, consolidating her notes. She was updating a to-do list for her assistant when her boss appeared.

"How did it go?"

Fiona smiled. "Client is happy."

Her boss's eyes narrowed. "And you?"

"I've never had to work with people who have no idea how television production works. David seems like a smart guy, but he's no producer, and the other guy looks like a hitman."

Her boss shrugged. "Is their money good?"

"Yes, the escrow account has over a million in it."

He clapped his hands. "Well then, let's keep them happy."

Jenny gently opened the door to her apartment and placed her gym bag on the floor. There was a broom leaning against the wall, and she grasped it in one hand as she hit the lights with the other.

"Buffalo, where are you, you little punk?"

Buffalo was her rescue cat, an athletic tabby whose mood was violently unpredictable. His favorite pastime was stalking her when she returned to their apartment.

She entered the living area and waited with the broom held high. The hairs on her neck rose as she heard a low growl from beneath the sofa.

"Buffalo, NO!" She braced herself for the onslaught.

He moved with lightning speed, a tiny tiger chasing down its prey. She swatted him away with the broom, and he skidded across the kitchen floor. "That's enough," she scolded, waving the broom.

He sprang onto the countertop as she opened the refrigerator and found his food. His tail lashed the marble surface, and he growled again.

Tearing the lid off a serving of fish, she slid the container across the bench. "There, happy?"

He sniffed the expensive dish, tasted it, and let out a cheerful meow.

"Bipolar little shit." She stroked his fur as he ate.

Buffalo continued eating as she took her meal from the freezer. She gave his dinner a sideways glance then scowled at hers. "Yeah, you definitely eat better than me." She threw the portion in the microwave and poured herself a glass of red wine.

Five minutes later, she sat on the couch with an average lasagna and a passable glass of wine. Before starting her dinner, she checked her phone and spotted an email reply from *The Operative*. Probably a 'thanks but no thanks.'

Sipping from her glass, she tapped on the message and was surprised to see she'd been selected for a spot at the Eastern Seaboard preliminary selection in Richmond, Virginia.

"Holy shit!" She immediately called Ben and told him the news.

"That's fantastic, babe. You have to do it," he replied.

"I don't know. What if I make it through to the next round? Who would look after Buffalo?"

"You do know that cat hates women, right? He'd be much happier chilling here with me."

She laughed. "That's true."

"So, no excuses. You're going to kick ass."

"Yeah," Jen said with trepidation. "Yeah, I guess I am."

Nick focused on the timer on his phone as the numbers counted down. His heart felt like it would burst from his chest and sweat ran off the Asian American's forehead like rain, hitting the treadmill's deck as his feet slapped it relentlessly.

The timer hit zero, and the belt slowed. Gasping for air, Nick grabbed a towel from the arm of the treadmill and wiped the sweat from his forehead.

Sprint training was something he did when he'd had a bad day. It was therapeutic, pushing himself till he nearly puked. Self-punishment for allowing people to walk all over him.

His pace had slowed to a fast jog when an alert popped up on his phone. It was a message from Magda. The elderly assistant so rarely messaged him that he'd forgotten she was the only person not screened by his do not disturb.

Poking his phone where it sat on the treadmill console, he unlocked the screen to see the message.

Way to go, James Bond. You got a spot.

For a split second, he had no idea what she meant. Then he remembered the reality TV show and the ten-page application he'd submitted. Excited, he grabbed the phone. Hands slick with sweat, it slipped through his fingers onto the treadmill deck. He sidestepped as it shot under him and slammed into his garage wall.

"Damn it." He punched the stop button and dismounted, recovering the device from the concrete floor. Thumbing the screen multiple times, he failed to get any response from the spider-webbed screen.

"You're kidding me."

He wandered out of the garage, through his modest

apartment and into his pokey office. Tossing the phone on his desk, he unlocked his laptop.

The alert from Magda was there too.

Opening his email account, he scrolled through the dozens of work messages, past one from his ex-wife and found the response from his application.

It was short, informing him that he'd been chosen for pre-selection for *The Operative*. While that didn't sound that impressive, it excited Nick. He hadn't won anything since college, much less been 'selected'. He pressed the accept button at the bottom of the email. It opened a webpage with the event's location and what to bring.

He'd never been to Virginia. Now all he had to do was convince his father to give him the day off. Even the thought of asking that made him nervous. Nope, he was going to call in sick. Not very James Bond, but at least he wouldn't have to deal with his father's scorn.

The Operative: Chapter Two

Vomit bubbled into Jen's mouth, but she managed to keep her lips closed and swallow it down as she dashed forward and threw herself across the line. The final siren blared, level fourteen of the beep test. Someone thrust a plastic cup of water into her hands, and she took it gratefully, using it to rinse the foul acidic taste from her mouth.

"Well done. You made it," the cheerful crew member announced. "Head over to the marquee for your next challenge."

Dragging herself to her feet, she glanced back at the contestants who hadn't been able to complete the fitness screening. The ordeal had consisted of a brutal strength circuit, Pilates session, mid-distance run, and finally, the ruthless beep test. She'd never worked so hard in her life.

Over a hundred hopefuls had turned up for the event, but over half hadn't made the grade. They now stood, pained, before a bubbly fitness instructor who thanked them for attending, while a film crew captured their anguish.

Meanwhile, those who had passed the fitness test were ushered into a large tent.

A camera and a microphone ambushed her as she entered.

"How are you feeling?" asked an interviewer.

"Exhausted," she managed. "One of the hardest physical activities I've ever done."

She contemplated pushing past but remembered this was a reality TV show selection. They would be looking for contestants who were engaging and charismatic.

"There was a point where I didn't think I would make it. So I dug deep and managed to get across the line."

"Any particular motivators?"

"Yeah, my nephews. I'm doing it for them."

"Great stuff. You better get going," said the producer. "We'll catch up with you if you pass the next phase."

The words didn't seem like much. But, the 'if' hit home. Throughout the day, Jenny noticed that many younger, fitter, better-looking contestants had been breezing through the fitness test. She'd barely scraped through, and no doubt, it would get much worse.

Tentatively, she joined the others in a briefing area and waited for instructions.

"Hopefully, that's the last of the beep tests. That nearly did me in," said the man next to her. Asian, middle-aged, and balding, he had an easy smile and friendly eyes.

"Glad I wasn't the only one," she replied.

"Not many people our age made it through. Hopefully, life experience can prevail over social media reach and rock-hard abs. My name's Nick."

"I'm Jen, a pleasure to meet you, Nick."

"You as nervous as I am?"

She nodded. "God knows what they're going to do to us next."

"Camera two. Zoom in on those oldies at the back. They look terrified." Charles Chen, *The Operative's* newly appointed director, issued his instructions via radio from the control center. "David, we're getting some great footage here. It's going to come together nicely."

Chen and a team of technicians were monitoring the footage from three roaming camera crews in the comfort of a purpose-built semi-trailer. David sat observing the proceedings from a plush couch opposite a wall of monitors.

The lawyer had run a full background check on Chen, and the lightly built Asian had come up clean. His family was from Taiwan; parents emigrated in the late eighties. He was born in ninety-four, attended good schools, and cut his teeth shooting action TV commercials in a top advertising firm. When he went out on his own, he achieved limited success, until he got a break directing an adventure reality TV show. Not that David cared about any of that. More importantly, Charles Chen's parents were deceased, and he had no partner or siblings. He was a loner.

"The next part may not be as interesting," said David.

Charles glanced at his run sheet. "Right, the psychological profiling and intelligence testing. We'll get some facial close-ups and chase down some interviews later. The audience will be more interested in the contestants' feelings than anything else."

"But, we can see the results live?" he asked.

"Andy?"

One of the technicians gestured to a screen where each contestant was listed. "As they input their answers on the tablets, their scores will update here. A green bar indicates success, and a red failure."

"Makes sense."

The door to the trailer swung open, and X stepped inside. The Chief Instructor wore his standard heavy-duty tan cargo pants and a T-shirt declaring *Coffee or Die*. Accordingly, he held two cups in one of his mammoth hands. He spotted David and passed him one.

"X, I want to introduce you to our director, Charles Chen," said David.

"People call me Chuck. So, your name's Ex? Like as in ex-wife?" The director offered his hand.

David snorted into his coffee.

The big man scowled, ignoring the handshake. "It's just X."

"Ah, like the letter. Right. Got it. So, how do you fit in?"

"He's a producer and the Chief Instructor. You do exactly as he says," said David.

Chuck frowned. "That's not how this works. I'm used to having full creative control."

"X isn't going to get in your way. He's here for authenticity," said David.

"Right, so you're the real deal," asked Chuck.

X smiled. "You do your thing, and I'll do mine."

"Cool, cool. Oh, and for future reference, I drink quad shot lattes." The director gave X a cheeky wink.

"Can you drink that through a straw?" X asked deadpan.

Chuck's brow rose. "Huh, straw?" He glanced at David, who clenched his fist and mimed a punch to the jaw.

Chuck swallowed and turned back to the screens. "I'll get the coffee next time."

"How are our numbers looking on the psychometrics?" asked X.

David gestured to the screen. Most of the names had green marks alongside them. "So far, so good."

"Let's see how many get through the challenge course," said X. "Then we'll know what we've got to work with."

The tower was at least three stories tall, with a wooden wall up one side against which a thick black rope hung. "I have to climb over that?" Jenny asked a male twenty-something fitness instructor.

"No, you climb the wall and then jump down."

"Jump?"

"That's what I said. Once you're back down, I'll give you the code."

"Can I look at the other side?"

The kid shook his head and pointed to the top of the tower.

Jenny moved across and grasped the rope. High above, she could see the top of the wooden wall. Remote cameras focused on her, attached to the frame.

Grasping the rope with both hands kept them from shaking. She swallowed and started pulling herself up the rope. Her muscles screamed with agony, and she kicked against the wall, taking some of the strain from her forearms and grip.

Halfway up, the only thing on her mind was fighting the urge to let go of the rope. The muscles in her arms had nothing left in them as she reached the top. She got a leg over the ledge and almost fell backward before rolling onto a narrow platform.

Her heart raced as she lay on her side, staring at the drop over the other side. Her stomach lurched as she rose to her knees and peered over the edge.

The bed of foam blocks looked like it was ten stories down. Jenny gripped a rail and stood as the instructor yelled from below.

"You've got two options. You can climb down the ladder and walk away from the competition. Or, you take the leap of faith."

So far, she'd completed tasks that ranged from navigating a maze blindfolded to folding an origami flower. Each time she finished, she'd earned a code. The drop below was her second last sequence to complete the challenge course.

She fought back panic as her legs nearly collapsed from under her.

"The ladder is right there," the instructor yelled.

Jenny heard the conceit in his voice.

Fuck you, she thought as she turned to one of the cameras. "I'm doing this for my nephews." She gripped the rail, took a deep breath, and let her body drop forward, rotating so that she landed back first into the bed of rubber squares.

"Well done!" yelled the PT from the side as he reached in and grabbed her hand. "That was awesome."

Jenny's heart pounded as he scrambled over the pit's edge and swung back to solid earth.

"Here's your code." He handed her a slip of paper. "You better get going."

Elation was quickly replaced with exhaustion as she ran through the parklands. She spotted a park bench through a gap in the trees and headed for it. Easing herself onto the wooden slats, she checked her watch. She had less than twenty minutes to reach her last challenge, complete it and make it to the finish line.

Examining her challenge map, she estimated it was at least another five hundred meters to her next task, then six hundred back to the finish. There was no way she could make it!

"Jenny!"

The voice startled her, seemingly coming from thick bushes. A second later, a figure emerged. It was the middle-aged man she'd met before the psychometric testing. She struggled to remember his name. "Nick?"

"Yeah, how's it going?" He made his way to the bench, looking worse for wear with a torn shirt and a coating of mud.

"Not good," she admitted. "I'm not going to make my last challenge at the lake."

"I just came from that. It's a hard one." He paused. "I'm in the same boat. I can't get to point eleven and back to the finish."

Jenny looked at her map. "I've just come from there."

There was an awkward silence.

Nick turned over his map and reread the rules. "There's nothing here about collaboration. It just says that contestants are to complete the activity on their own. It could be argued that we're achieving that as long as we cross the finish line apart."

Jenny frowned. "Are you a lawyer?"

Nick laughed. "As a matter of fact. Look, we've got nothing to lose. We're not going to make the timings as it is. You can be sure that the millennial crowd will have gotten them all done."

Jenny nodded. Fit athletes had passed her more than once in the last few hours. "What if the codes are different?"

Nick shook his head. "You've seen the kids running this thing. They'll be different for each activity, but that's it. Trust me, I know human nature."

Jenny checked her watch. She had even less time now. There was no way they were going to complete the task. Nick was right, there was only one option. She passed him the slip of paper from the wall. "This is your last one."

He did the same, and she scribbled the combination into the box on her map.

"I'll give you a head start," said Nick. "See you at the finish."

Grab your copy...
vinci-books.com/silkstone-operative

About the Author

Jack Silkstone grew up on a steady diet of Tom Clancy, James Bond, Jason Bourne, *Commando* comics, and the original first-person shooters, *Wolfenstein* and *Doom*. His background includes a career in military intelligence and special operations, working alongside some of the world's most elite units. His love of action-adventure stories, his military background, and his real-world experiences combined to inspire the no-holds-barred PRIMAL series.

www.ingramcontent.com/pod-product-compliance
Ingram Content Group UK Ltd.
Pitfield, Milton Keynes, MK11 3LW, UK
UKHW040118190326
469155UK00004B/1220